I0522902

PortaL to EarthA

E.E. Rawls

PORTAL TO EARTHA.
Copyright © by author E.E. Rawls 2020
All rights reserved

Cover art by H.S.J. Williams

This is a work of fiction. Names, characters, businesses, places, events, locales, and incidents are either the products of the author's imagination or used in a fictitious manner. Any resemblance to actual persons, living or dead, or actual events is purely coincidental.

Associated logos and art are trademarks of author E.E. Rawls. All characters, story world and elements are copyright by E.E. Rawls.

This book or any portion thereof
may not be reproduced or used in any manner whatsoever
without the express written permission of the publisher
except for the use of brief quotations in a book review.

ISBN 978-0-9985569-4-9

www.eerawls.com

Printed in the U.S.A.
First edition, November 2020

Titles by E.E. Rawls

Earthaverse:

~ ⚬ ~

DRAEV GUARDIANS SERIES

Strayborn (1)

Dragons & Ravens (1.5)

Strayblood (2)

Alteredverse:

~ ⚬ ~

Frost, Winter's Lonely Guardian

Portal to Eartha

Beast of the Night

Madness Solver in Wonderland

Coming Soon:

Straypath (3)

Secret projects ;)

Find out when the next books are releasing, and get
exclusive content, by following my newsletter at:
eerawls.com

To those who seek,
for you will find.

Prologue

2110 AD

Lotus gazed up at the pendant her dad held aloft. Its crystal facets topped by metallic green leaves sparkled in the lamplight.

"Long, long, *very long* ago," spoke Dad, making her giggle as he recited the old story that had been passed down from generation to generation in their family, "back when humankind was still recovering from the Great Flood that had decimated the lands, people began to build new kingdoms across the face of the Earth. But the work was difficult and long, and the humans became more and more dissatisfied with their slow progress day by day. Soon, their impatience and temper reached a boiling point, and they went and did what humans do best: they complained.

"They saw how the animals, birds and other creatures adapted so easily to their environments and how they never seemed troubled or hindered by anything. With their wings they were able to travel anywhere, with their claws able to dig up anything, and with their strength able to hunt down any prey. The humans grumbled and complained, for their bodies were weak and fragile in comparison to these creatures.

"Their grumbling and whining continued day after day, month after month, *year* after *year*, until finally the heavens parted and an angel was sent down to speak with them.

"'Why have you given us such a pathetic form?' some of the humans cried out. 'We toil away, while an animal can do in one day what would take us weeks. We have no claws to help us plant our fields, no wings to help us travel from place to place, no strength of a bear to bring down a hunt with ease. Why have you made us so weak?'

"They complained on and on through the angel to Lord God about how unfair this all was."

Lotus clapped her hands to the sides of her head, as if all the imagined complaining were making her ears hurt. Dad chuckled and continued the tale.

"God, in His great patience, heard their plea, and He sent down to Earth a grove of trees. This special grove grew on a remote island, and the trees there bore strange and colorful fruit.

"The angel told them that each tree's fruit would grant them a different gift, and so, they must choose wisely what it was they wished for and not complain about the results afterwards—for this was their own doing.

"Now, the humans who had complained and were not satisfied with how God had made them, went to the trees, and each chose a fruit and then ate.

"In that moment their bodies were transformed: some subtly, others drastically. Humans who ate of the flight trees were given feathers and wings; those who ate of the earth trees were given claws and tools for digging and living underground; those who ate of the strength trees were given a wide variety of animal characteristics and heightened senses.

"There were many trees, and many changes. This is how goblins, elves, kitsune, hauks, and vempars (like you and me), and many more races were born," said Dad.

"But when these transformed humans returned to the mainland and to their fellow humans, they were feared and shunned for their strange new appearances. The humans named those who had eaten of the trees: the Altered Ones, and they separated themselves from them.

"The Altered soon realized their mistake. For humankind was not as weak as they had once thought, but growing in intelligence and technology, and able to accomplish feats which no animal could. But it was too late, and the Altered could not change back.

"As the years passed, humans populated the planet, and the Altered lagged behind, few in number. Our kind was discriminated against, feared, banned from areas, and even hunted down.

"We lived in fear of humans for ages…until one group of brave Altered banded together to work towards a solution: they named themselves the Beorgan Society."

"Burger Society!" Lotus interjected.

Dad tickled her foot. She laughed, trying to roll out of his reach.

"*Beor-gan*. Listen up, kid. This secret society busied itself searching for a solution, a way to find peace. And when one of their members sought the advice of a great Nymph who dwelled in the caves of Japan, after much discussion, the Nymph was persuaded to help the endangered Altered in their plight.

"The Nymph revealed the existence of a portal within his caves that led to another world—a world where Altered could dwell in peace and prosper. A planet similar to ours: Eartha, the second Earth.

"The Beorgan Society gathered brilliant Altered in all scientific fields, bringing them to the portal where they worked together to construct a stabilizer around the portal, making it wider and more stable. They then spread the message through secret channels across the globe: that those who wanted a new life, separate from humans, should come to the designated cave without delay, and there the Society would meet them. On a set date, everyone who gathered to the cave would walk through the portal and leave the old world behind.

"The message spread, and the date drew near, and the Beorgan Society took precautions as they gathered Altered together in groups. Once the date arrived, a mass exodus of Altered left for Eartha. They entered a new world and a new beginning, finally free.

"The members of the society were the last to leave, and they left behind clues for those Altered who had chosen to stay behind, should things grow worse one day and they, too, needed to flee. This," Dad jingled the pendant, "is said to be one of those clues."

Lotus cocked her head and squinted one eye at the crystal.

"This pendant has been passed down for many centuries in our family, with the story being that a map lies somewhere inside it: showing the way to the portal for any who seek to escape this world. Much has been forgotten over the years, but our ancestors were entrusted with this secret. And it's why we moved here, to Japan, to the land said to contain this specific portal."

"Are we going to the portal?"

Dad grunted. "I wish we could. But that pendant refuses to show me the map. I've tried everything! It's stubborn about keeping its secret."

"Wow, even a rock can outsmart you. That's really sad, Dad."

"Hush, is not! I'm very smart."

"Let Mom look at it."

"Why do kids always assume their mom is smarter? She's already looked at it, you know, and can't no more figure it out than I can!"

Lotus stretched up on her legs. She peered out a window and gasped suddenly. "The sun's almost at noon. We gotta leave, now, or the circus show will end before we get there!"

"Lotus, are you sure seeing the circus is so important?" Hesitation lined Dad's voice, and she gave him a look. "We avoid going into the village for a reason," he furthered.

"Avoid going *anywhere*, you mean. I'm tired of the same hills and trees, and not having any friends. My life is weird because we're vempars, I know; bad humans could find us if we're not careful. But I'm so bored! Dad, all I'm asking for is one trip—*one trip* just to see the circus while it's nearby."

Dad scrubbed his face with a hand. "Go put on your hat, then."

Lotus shot her arms up in a cheer and tugged on a big blue hat to hide her pointy ears. Mom shared a skeptical glance with Dad, before they both likewise put on hats, tucking in their ears.

After a long walk past rolling fields and terraced rice paddies, the village came into view.

Lotus skipped down the dirt street—lined with booths and stalls and hanging red lanterns—ahead of her parents. A crowd was already forming, and she pushed her way through to the open village center where the performance had set up and was already in progress.

A man and woman dressed in silky body suits twirled lit torches, making fire spin patterns in the air, searing after-images into the crowd's eyes.

An older man in a blue kimono made his way along the front of the ringing crowd, gait swaying as he held a venomous snake for all to marvel at. Its brown scales reflected the flames as he passed by Lotus.

"And now, for our next act!" the circus leader shouted from the sidelines. "It's a sight rarely seen—so rare, in fact, that it has become the stuff of fairy tales and ancient myth. Hold on to your wigs and fans, ladies and gents, so they won't be blown away," he warned dramatically. Then he thrust an arm out and called, "Come forth, our Daring Falcon!"

There was a whoosh of air from the parked circus trailer, and a shadow soared across the sky above the crowd: the outline of wings, and a figure attached to them.

Daring Falcon soared over the crowd's heads as people gasped in fright and awe. Lotus tried to see how the wings were attached to the figure, a young boy, but there was no device holding them in place. And the wings were real wings—you couldn't fake something like that, the way they maneuvered in the air, yet no predatory bird existed with wings that large.

"An Altered. How rare," Mom whispered at her side, having caught up, and Lotus tipped her head back to watch.

"Like us?" Lotus followed the shape in the sky.

The boy was soaring free and gracefully above the air currents—untouchable, and relishing every minute of it. His hair, a mix of charcoals and whites like a falcon's feathers, rippled; his skin a creamy brown.

"What kind of Altered is he?" she asked.

"Judging by the wing colors, I'd say the hauk race. Rare for Japan," said Mom.

"Toss the hoops!" rang a shout, and two other performers carried a series of metal hoops in different sizes out onto the clearing that was their stage.

The largest hoop was thrown high.

Daring Falcon plunged in a downward arc: through the hoop and out—so quickly that if she'd blinked, she would have missed it.

Three hoops were tossed at once, each smaller than the next, and the Falcon boy tilted his wings forward and back, undulating up and down like a dolphin through each hoop.

The crowd gave applause.

"It doesn't end there, ladies and gentlemen. Bring forth the Rings of Fire!"

Yanking on thick gloves, the performers put matches to a series of hoops and then threw them high.

Blazing rings of fire filled the sky, and Daring Falcon swooped to go through, tucking his wings in at the last second; first through one hoop, then the next, then a smaller one…

He spread his wings to gain more momentum before closing them tightly and shooting through the smallest hoop, barely fitting.

The crowd cheered as he came out the other side. But Lotus could see that the tips of his feathers were singed. That last hoop was too dangerous.

The act now finished, the boy glided back toward the circus trailer, his back slumped as if a leash were pulling him down from the sky he loved to the bleak ground. He shouldn't be doing that crazy stunt, getting himself burned, she thought. Didn't he know better? And why did he look so sad?

"Mom, I want to go to the trailer and meet him."

"Lotus, no." Mom's gaze widened a fraction, and she caught her arm to stop her. "Don't go anywhere near there, you hear me? It's not safe."

"Why?" Lotus snapped back.

Why couldn't she even talk with a fellow Altered her own age?

Dad leaned close enough to whisper, "That boy is owned by the circus. He's like a slave, Lotus. That's what can happen to Altered who get found out—that and worse."

Lotus stilled.

Daring Falcon was a slave? That could happen to any of them—even to her?

Lotus's stomach turned queasy. "I want to go home," she said, even as the next circus act began.

Dad nodded and hugged an arm around her shoulders as they headed back.

Dad bent his arms, and the pendant necklace lowered to Lotus's chest. "Today, our family secret is passed down to you," he announced, and he fastened the clasp.

Lotus admired the sparkling crystal and shiny metal leaves, twirling it between her fingers.

Somewhere within was a map—a map that could lead them to a better place, a world where boys with wings didn't become slaves, and girls with fangs and pointy ears didn't have to live in hiding from civilization.

"I'll find the secret map, Dad. Don't you worry!"

He chuckled and tousled her orange curls. "I know you will."

His own curly hair matched hers. She'd always liked that, having the same hair; like another family heirloom that would always be passed down.

Lotus opened the sliding door and dashed outside: into the evening light and the sprawling field, at the end of which were the rows of rice paddies and muddy water that they worked.

"Mom, look! See what I got!" she called.

Her bare feet squished in the grass, then in the soggy soil the farther she went. The strands of her wild orange hair whipped in the breeze around her shoulders.

"Mom?"

Where was she? She wanted to show her! The necklace was finally hers to wear!

Lotus followed the horizon line with her eyes, across the paddy field and up the tall hills jutting to either side. A forest of lanky bamboo trees swayed off to her right.

Maybe Mom had sat down in the shade after tending the rice?

As Lotus made her way over, the field grew eerily silent. Crickets and cicadas stilled their never-ending serenade.

She wanted to call out again, but a strange feeling kept her quiet. She stepped under the canopy, and a breeze whooshed past and clattered the bamboo trunks together like massive wood chimes.

"Mom...?" she whispered to the air.

Something brown peeked out from behind a tangled cluster of bamboo shoots, and Lotus's face lit up.

"Mom!" She dashed around the stalks to her mom's brown hair and white yukata garment. Mom sat there with her attention focused on the ground.

"Look at this. Dad finally gave me the old heirloom! It's—" She paused.

Mom wasn't listening, still tipping her face down to the ground.

"Look." She bent low and jingled the necklace so that the sound would pique interest. Yet still, Mom didn't look up.

"Why are you ignoring me?" She sat on her knees and grabbed Mom's shoulder to shake it. Then saw something protruding from her chest, red dripping out. Mom's stare was glazed and fixed down at nothing.

Lotus screamed.

Mom was…was…

It looked like a spear, angled through the heart.

Lotus fell backwards and clawed at the damp soil to get back up. "Dad! Dad, help!!" She scrambled to get out of the bamboo forest. "Dad!"

Just as she reached the open field, gun shots echoed from the house.

She halted, pointy ears twitching. When there was trouble, the drill was to seek the nearest designated hiding place and stay there. But Mom was…this couldn't be happening. She had to reach Dad. He had to be okay!

Her feet pounded and squished in the moist ground, heading for the house.

She spotted a thin figure with a head of tawny-orange curls exit one of the doors. "Dad!"

The *amado* wall behind him suddenly broke apart. She watched in horror as a hulking body crashed out of the house, arms out, firing guns. Dad ducked under the shots and ran into the large gunman's knees, knocking him down.

Dad turned, and his eyes met hers as she stopped short of reaching the house. "Run!" he shouted.

"But Mom—!"

"Don't argue with me, *go!*" He waved, his expression stern though edged with fear.

"Dad…" Tears blurred her vision.

The gunman rose, and other footsteps and shapes came from around the other side of the house.

"GO!" Dad fought to knock the gunman back down, and other shots fired from the guns of those approaching. Some must have hit, because Dad sunk to his knees, still fighting to drag the first man down. The people with guns weren't just humans: she saw grayish green skin and warts, jagged and twisted ears—goblins.

He couldn't fight them all, she realized, even with his vempar strength. He was just buying her time.

Dad landed a knock-out punch to the man, then barreled into a second. More shots fired and Dad didn't dodge but used his speed to crash through one gunman after another, wrenching guns away and dealing rock-hard fist blows.

She should have run, but she wanted to see that Dad would be okay. She couldn't just leave.

A large shape burst out of the house's door: a trollic—a tusked beast like the old Japanese depictions of demons.

Dad finished a punch before turning at the sound. A spear thrust from the trollic's hands, and Lotus screamed as it struck Dad through the chest. The trollic gave a twisted grin of pleasure.

Dad gripped the haft, clawing at it, weakly trying to pull it out; but between the trollic's strength and the many injuries already bleeding his body, Dad was losing the fight. He turned his head slightly, not quite facing her, though she knew the words his lips mouthed were for her: *I'm sorry.*

The attackers' attention turned to her. Dad slumped forward, and she ran.

She headed for the forest-covered hills, using every ounce of vempar strength in her legs to propel her, barely able to see through the curtain of tears, barely able to breathe through her tight chest.

The trees came nearer, nearer, her feet sloshing through the rice paddies.

Something lashed painfully around her knees and made her fall suddenly. She scrambled on her palms and yanked at the strange rope that had somehow bound her legs, panic making her movements clumsy.

Heavy, sloshing steps came up behind her, just as a shot fired and a second rope caught her neck, wrapping itself around her. She couldn't breathe. Her fingers clawed at it as little to no air reached her lungs.

The field blurred, hazed, and darkened.

1

SWEAT TRICKLED DOWN HER brow as she concentrated on the knife wound.

Sixteen-year-old Lotus channeled a flow of life-energy down her arm, through her hand and into the wound pressed beneath it. The super-cells unique to vempars seeped from her palm and began Healing the damaged flesh.

After several minutes, she withdrew her hand, and the burly, gruff man sat upright, twisting to eye the now-gone stab wound in his side.

"*Mirakuru*, it's really gone. Just like magic!"

She hated doing this.

"That's right, *chinpira*. Now get back to your job," said Shiro, her bodyguard—or more accurately, her jailor.

He pulled the thug by the elbow and shoved him out the door, before letting the next man who stood in line enter the room.

Not as long of a line today—thank goodness. Healing these undeserving wretches of the underground world never got any easier on her conscious. But she was the property of the Kuro Mafia, here, in Fukuoka City. Brought and bought for only one reason: to make a profit off her vempar gift of Healing.

The mafia's thugs and followers were Healed of injuries acquired from their dangerous work and odious deeds, while others, not related to the mafia, who heard the rumors of Healing came pouring in for the service—and paying a hefty sum to get it.

Even after years of doing this, she still couldn't get used to seeing nasty gashes and bullet wounds, and having to knit together almost-severed appendages.

"Get your head out of your thoughts, Lotus."

Shiro's impatient growl made her rise and bow politely to the next customer, before seating them down on the bench. This man had a blade wound across the chest that had become infected.

She sucked in a breath, then started in again on the only work she knew how to do.

Lotus yawned into her elbow and finished washing her hands in the medic's room. It was late morning and time for her shift to end. Shiro tapped his shiny heel against the wall behind him, waiting.

The mafia's crew—or whatever you wanted to call them— did their dirty work from dusk into the early dawn hours, which meant that her day consisted of night hours as jobs went wrong and people needed Healing.

"Spending an hour cleaning those nails isn't gonna make you pretty," Shiro said.

"No, but it lets me forget what I'm forced to do for a living every day," she muttered.

"A living?" He laughed at that, coughing on a cigar. She was no better than a slave—she didn't make *a living*. "Before you go making me choke and die of laughter, you ought to know I'll be away on another job, starting tomorrow, for a few weeks." She dried her hands. "Another fella's gonna be escorting you around."

"A substitute jailor? Who knew they did that?"

"Heh. Careful, he may be too much for even your sense of humor to handle." Shiro tossed the cigar and stamped on it. "Ready?" He went out the door before she could answer, and she trotted after him.

The underground district was quiet at this hour. Lotus tipped her head back at the ceiling's swirling metal patterns and dimmed lights. The series of tunnels and stores had once been an underground shopping mall, but now it was the place of dark business dealings, ruled by the mafia. She rarely got to go outside the tunnels—the customers came to her, here, where she could be secured.

What shade of blue was the sky, again? Memories of the rice paddy farm were faded, what grass felt like beneath her feet a distant life belonging to someone else.

She and Shiro passed walls of glass windows filled with illegal merchandise and halted at the exotic butcher's shop. "Oi, Karlo!" Shiro kicked the metal base of the register booth, making it clang.

A rotund head peeked out from the back. The man grumbled something in Japanese, and after several minutes emerged with his live catch for the day: a tied up wild boar and three caged hares. Lotus glanced down with pity at what would be her victims.

Rotund Karlo kept a noticeable distance between himself and her as she bent down, reaching her hand to touch the boar. It wheezed and growled but couldn't do much tied up. In a way, the animal was like her, except she wore a tracking collar.

The boar's body pulsed with energy, and she drew that life-energy into her palm, soaking it up and replenishing her own body with it. Vempars needed life-energy to survive; but when she took it from animals, it made her nauseous and weary.

When she lifted her hand, the boar was dead, and Karlo hauled it back into his butcher shop where it would become tomorrow's specialty. She turned to the hares, doing the same, and hating herself all the while. Caught animals had no chance to run, no chance to survive.

Shiro was tapping his foot impatiently.

Done, she sank to her knees as her stomach fought off nausea and her head spun. After a while, the feeling faded, and they continued the tunnel trek, up to one particular store lined with bars like a jail.

Shiro unlocked the door before navigating through a series of rooms inside, stopping once they reached hers. She yawned as he locked the door behind her, then she flopped onto the platform bed and stiff pillow.

Lotus fished for the miPod under the blanket and plugged the earphones in her ears. A button made the thin, folded frame open and turn on. Scrolling through the air inside the frame, she found the latest soothing dubstep album and let the light techno drift her away into sleep.

"The members of the Society were the last to leave, and they left behind clues for those Altered who had chosen to stay behind, should things grow worse one day and they, too, needed to flee. This is said to be one of those clues."

Dad's words.

The pendant with its dangling crystal rotated, light reflecting off its numerous facets, the green metal leaves cupping it like a flower.

"A map lies somewhere inside it: showing the way to the portal for any who seek to escape this world."

Escape this world…

Lotus sat up, awake, shoving the blanket aside and blinking in the darkness.

She reached for the nightlight, then slumped back against the wall, touching the pendant that dangled beneath her shirt, always kept close to her heart.

"A map to the portal…is it real? Could there be such a thing?" she spoke aloud to the dark. "If there really is, will you show me, Lord God?"

She watched her faint shadow on the wall, the crystal rotating on its chain.

Who was she kidding? She couldn't escape the Kuro Mafia. They made big money off of her Healing and had put a tracking collar on her neck to keep it that way. Even if she did somehow manage to get away and lose the collar, she'd need to find sources of life-energy every day to stay alive; and she'd have to escape the notice of other humans who might kidnap her, as the mafia had.

It wasn't just one group or one city that was the enemy — the whole world was full of enemies eager to kill her or use her. She understood that now, what her parents had been protecting her from.

Was it that day in the village, watching the circus perform, that had sealed their fate and allowed the wrong people to find her and her family?

"Dad…Mom…" She let the tears wet her cheeks.

Dad would have told her it wasn't her fault, that all things happened for a reason. But she would always carry some guilt in her heart.

The crystal was smooth between her fingertips as she rolled it back and forth, except for one facet that rubbed bumpy along her thumb—centuries of encrusted grime, probably.

"Is this all my life will ever be?"

Trapped. Used. Shouldering guilt.

She tried to recall the serene night sky and myriads of stars back at the farm, the moments of stargazing with her dad and chasing fireflies with her mom.

2

THE HARSH CLANG OF A KEY and then a fist knocking on the door jolted Lotus awake. She tugged on a t-shirt, jeans and jacket, brushed her curly tangle of orange hair, brushed her teeth, and grabbed for a protein bar, before Shiro on the other side of the door grew impatient and knocked even louder.

What was with him? She always took some time to get ready—that's why he came ten minutes early to wake her up! It was—

She looked at the electric clock: It was already time for her to be in the clinic room. Shiro hadn't given her any time at all!

She chewed on the bar, which had a fake chocolate taste, and stuffed her feet into sneakers while the knocking persisted.

"YOU'RE MAKING US LATE."

Her hand stilled on the doorknob. That wasn't Shiro's voice. It wasn't even a voice at all.

Then she remembered what Shiro had said, that he'd be away for the week.

But…what sort of person had a robot for a voice?

Lotus gingerly turned the knob and creaked open the door, one eye peeking through the gap. She caught an angry green gaze before the door suddenly shoved open and the young man behind it towered over her.

"GET GOING."

He was a strange sight—and she'd seen plenty of strange sights in the underground business. Layered hair a mix of charcoals and whites around a brown face, dark circles under the eyes; a thin frame dressed in black, with a cape that bulged abnormally from his back; and leather gloves that his hands kept fidgeting with. When he turned his head, she saw that some of the hair at the nape of his neck was feathers.

"GO." His lips didn't move.

She had to blink several times. A device attached to the side of his face looped back behind his head and plugged into both ears—and it was speaking for him.

Well, that explained the robot voice.

"So, you're the new jailor?" she said. "I'm Lotus. Nice to meet you."

The man's blank stare and neutral lips didn't change.

"It's polite to give your name," she tried again, but he turned to leave the door. "Oh, come on. Is there a name you'd like me to use for you? Otherwise, it'll be Lollipop."

She followed him out, through the halls and rooms. "Okay then, Lollipop it is," she said at his back. "Tomorrow, give me an extra ten minutes to get ready—that's what my other jailor does."

She followed him along the underground tunnel network in silence, the ceiling lights brightening as evening came on and businesses woke up for the night's work.

"Well, you're just a bundle of fun, aren't you?" she muttered. She again noted the odd way Lollipop's cape bumped out as he walked, almost like it was hiding something.

Reaching the clinic and medic room, Lotus tied her hair back and wrapped on an apron before the evening stream of customers were allowed in. The evening crowd consisted of ordinary people who had heard rumors of Healing, and out of desperation came to take a chance that it might be true—and to pay the hefty fee. They were easier to Heal because they weren't all thugs and bullies. Some were even children, and it was that part that made living here a tad more bearable.

Midnight approached, and Lotus sat back, pressing the back of her hand to her forehead, massaging it. "So, Lollipop, what's your story? How'd you end up in this mafia joint?"

The young man hadn't said a word all evening. She couldn't stand not talking. Shiro used to indulge her with conversation: about the latest city news, the wet weather, the many stupid ways in which people spent their money—*anything*. But the silence with this guy was racking her nerves.

"Maybe you're a bad conversation starter? Fine, here's a topic: Have the cherry trees in the great beyond above bloomed yet?"

He turned his head a fraction, almost looking at her, then turned back to the door where no more customers waited.

"If it's the robot voice stopping you, don't worry about it. I could talk to a microwave and be happy, just as long as it says something back."

He snorted.

Was that a reaction? Finally! He was communicating!

Even if it was just guttural.

"So, how about it? Are the trees all happy and abloom with spring? I'd love to find some excuse to go up and see them for myself. I can't remember the last time I saw flowers during the day. Maybe, at dawn, you and I could sneak up for a peek?"

No reaction. He was blank ice again.

She heaved a grumbling sigh and sat back in a chair, stretching her limbs out and getting more impatient by the second. Another customer had better come through and be talkative, or else she'd go crazy.

Beep-beep-beep.

Her pointy ears perked as Lollipop answered the call and held up his comm watch, wrapped over his leather sleeve, to his ear:

"There's a big shoot-out happening at Block 15. Many of our guys are down. Bring that Healer over here, hayaku!"

Lotus's heartbeat quickened.

"HAI," the young man's robot voice replied, and he put down his wrist and faced her.

But she waved her hand. "I heard; vempars have sharp hearing, you know. Guess I'll get my wish to go outside, now."

Lotus chucked off the apron and followed him out the clinic store. If only it were daylight so she could see the pink flower colors, enjoy a pleasant excursion instead of entering a bloody shoot-out.

Oh well. One can't have everything.

Lotus zipped her jacket as they exited through one of several exit doors in the underground tunnels—all of them monitored—and scaled the flight of stairs up to the ground surface.

A vacuum of air whipped at her hair, and the scent of freshness and rain filled her nose and caressed her cheeks. It struck her how much she'd missed this, the feel of outdoors.

The stairs opened to the city world above. Lights and bright signs flashed, a roaring commotion of sleek cars and pedestrians and random music filled the air. Colorful characters danced on the screens of sky-rising buildings.

Lotus stepped out from under the stair awning and into the drizzled air. She crossed to a sidewalk where one tree stood in full bloom. She took in the pink hue of the petals lit by the city lights and stuffed her nose in one flower, breathing in sweetness.

"*NO TIME.*" The jailor caught her by the hood of her jacket, pulling her along.

"Oh, now you speak?" She twisted out of his grip. "*Stop and smell the roses* is a good saying for cooped up people like me. So let me smell them, will you?"

"*DO YOU WANT TO BE CARRIED OR DRAGGED THERE?*" His gaze was almost withering.

She grumbled and trotted after him down a less-crowded sidewalk. "Someone's robot voice needs a tune-up. For sounding bland, it's sure got attitude."

People became scarce the closer they drew to Block 15. That is, until the pop of guns and smoke of fume bombs filled the air.

The same voice shouted again through the jailor's comm watch, but they had already reached the Block.

"*KEEP LOW,*" the jailor instructed Lotus, and his gloved hand pushed her head down so that she crouched when she didn't listen fast enough. "*STAY CLOSE BEHIND ME.*"

"I'm a vempar—not some defenseless human!"

He ducked into an alley beside a restaurant, and from there approached the sound of gunfire. At a concrete corner, he motioned behind for her to stop. *"I'LL BRING THE INJURED HERE FOR YOU TO HEAL."*

Lotus frowned, but he was already off: crouching around the corner and dashing into the street. His cape flapped back as he moved, and she glimpsed feathers underneath. She gaped and blinked after he'd gone.

Feathers? Who would have feathers under their cape? The nape of his neck had feathers, too. Was it some new gangster statement that she didn't know about?

Seconds ticked by, and she pressed her shoulder against the alley wall of a crumbling building. This must be a serious shoot-out involving important members for the Kuro Mafia to risk bringing her out. The tracking collar kept her under their boot, but she could rip it off and run. With her strength, she could do it. But without a place to go or hide, mafia members or someone worse would track her down—and then they'd make her life far worse than it already was.

Lotus breathed in the mist rising off the pavement and flinched at a series of loud gun shots nearby and the stench of smoke. Running was tempting, but Fukuoka was a big city with nowhere friendly for an Altered to hide. She was afraid to leave, she realized. Afraid of what worse things could be out there, of the stories of caught Altered and their fates that made her job pale in comparison. She shuddered.

A shadow traveled across the wall opposite the corner, followed by something scraping. She tensed, then saw it was Lollipop dragging a burly man. She kneeled and had a look at the bullet wounds as the jailor left to find others.

She concentrated and Healed the most vital wounds first, pushing the bullets out. Another wounded gunman was brought, and as a third stumbled into the alley, the jailor was

holding his side and sinking to a crouch to rest against the wall while she worked.

Once each person had been mended, she turned her attention to him. "What kind of jailor are you, getting yourself shot? Sit," she ordered.

His mouth pressed in a frown, then the pain convinced him to sit and let her have a look.

She shoved the cape out of the way and pulled the jacket up to see: the shot had gone clean through and out, just enough to the side not to have hit anything vital. She pressed her hand against him, and he gave a slight grunt at her touch. With the cape shifted aside, she could clearly see the feathers hidden beneath: a wing like that of a hawk.

A sound of surprise escaped her lips. Once she removed her hand, he quickly pulled the cape close as if it were something to hide. He was an Altered, like her.

He rose to leave and look for more wounded, ignoring her plea that he wait until the fighting was over. For someone who didn't talk much, this guy was stubborn. He edged towards the corner.

She sat back on her heels to wait. Then a shadow not connected to either of them moved.

She turned her neck to find the barrel of a gun staring down at her.

Her mouth opened, too late to cry out. The gun fired.

She squinted, ears ringing. The jailor gripped the barrel, having shoved its aim away, and dealt one swift uppercut to the wielder's jaw.

The gunman toppled. Lollipop had just saved her from a lot of pain and Healing. Her breath misted the air before her as she glanced up at him. He was just doing his job, but she could fantasize, right? He *was* easy on the eyes.

It wasn't long before police sirens arrived, and he turned back to her. Those she'd Healed were hurrying off down the opposite alley to waiting cars.

The comm watch beeped and an urgent voice crackled through: *"Toshi, get the Healer here to the base, pronto! The boss's son has been hit."*

Lotus went wide-eyed. "The boss's…?"

But the jailor had her wrist and was pulling her along up a side alley and out to the street where the last car waited. Getting inside, the car's engine hummed, speeding them away.

"Toshi, hm? I kinda liked Lollipop, though it does take more effort to say," Lotus observed. "How's your wing doing? The feathers look rather beat up. I could fix that for you."

He jerked away and focused on the opposite window, clearly not wanting to discuss it. Had there only been one wing? She couldn't be sure from the brief look she'd had.

Arriving at the base of Kuro Mafia's operations—at one of the city's most expensive and soaring buildings—Lotus was ushered inside. They took her up the glass elevator; drizzle condensed upon the glassy view of the large city bathed in night.

It had been years since she'd seen the boss of the group that had purchased her from kidnappers. Her heart started beating faster. One wrong move and he could have her whipped, tortured, or worse. He owned her, and she felt the weight of it.

The elevator doors opened, and Lotus found herself hurried into a wide flat, filled with all the wealth and modern décor you would expect to find in the home of a billionaire. There, laid out on a sofa, was a human in his thirties, blood soaking down the cushions, his father standing over him.

She reached the son's side and unbuttoned his shirt to see the wounds they'd tried to wrap and keep pressure on.

It was bad. Very bad. Five gun shots to the chest, and the son was barely breathing. But it was the last bullet hole that made her go still; it had severed a major artery, and he was bleeding from it non-stop.

Lotus placed her hands over the artery, but knew it was too late. Even as it Healed, the man's breathing fell still—he'd lost too much blood.

"What are you doing? Heal him!" the wide-set boss, Kuro, shouted.

She flinched. "He's already gone, sir. I'm sorry. We were too late."

"Don't tell me lies, you filth! Keep Healing him!" The boss's face and double-chin bloated red with rage.

She kept Healing, though it was pointless; nothing could create new blood for him. He should have been taken to a hospital instead of carried here.

"I said, Heal him!" Kuro practically screamed at her.

She cringed as her ears rang. "I did! He's still gone!"

Meaty hands grabbed her shoulders and shoved her into the sofa, hitting her head on the wood part of the armrest. "Use the Healing Kiss! And don't tell me you can't do it—I *know* every vempar can."

Lotus sucked on her bleeding lip and righted herself. The Healing Kiss was the last resort, the only way to Heal someone who had died, but it would only work within minutes of the person's death…and it cost the life of the vempar who used it.

The boss was willing to lose future profits from her if it meant bringing back his son.

But Lotus wasn't ready to die. Her parents hadn't tried to raise her and keep her safe just so she would end up like this, dying to save a son that was just as bad a criminal as his father.

Lotus shook her head and stood. "You're asking me to die."

"I'm *telling* you to die! Bring back my son." Kuro lunged for her, and she dodged to the other side of the sofa. "Grab her!"

The two bodyguards with him came at her from both sides. She punched the first, but the second grabbed her arms from behind in a lock hold, and the first one joined him. They held her in front of the son, and the boss unsheathed a long knife to rest across her neck. "Either die saving him or die by my knife severing your head. Choose!"

The edge cut a line across her skin, and Lotus tried not to flinch. Every inch of her body trembled.

"He died of blood loss. No amount of Healing can bring him back," her voice wavered against the knife. "Healing can't create blood. He needs a blood transfusion, first." A partial lie, and one she hoped Kuro would buy.

The knife brushed along her skin. Kuro turned to the lackey standing by the door, "How fast can a blood transfusion be set up here?"

"The hospital isn't far. We can pay off one of the nurses. But it'd be faster to bring Kuro Junior there with us, instead of driving all the way back here with equipment."

Kuro exhaled. "*Tcheh*. Get to it, then!"

The lackey scurried off, and Lotus sucked in a breath. She glanced at Toshi, who was still near the door and impossible to read.

This would be her only chance.

As a stretcher was brought in, and the son carried out, the guards kept a tight grip on her, and the whole group filed out to the elevator.

She struggled to breathe evenly as they came out the building and over to a large waiting black van.

The lackeys and Kuro were busy for a moment fitting the stretcher into the back of the van, and it was in that moment that Lotus unleashed her vempar strength: ripping her arms from the guards' hold and somersaulting up to land behind them and deal two powerful punches to the backs of their heads that sent them reeling, unconscious.

Lotus ran with inhuman speed down the street in the opposite direction.

The shouts after her soon faded, and the rush of air and patter of light rain took over. She dove down street after street, and wove through alley after alley, until the pavement paths were a blur and neon signs flashed all around.

She was running away. Was this really happening?

The collar—she had to get it off. She bit down on her arm where a micro-chip had been implanted, ripping it out.

Digging her fingers around the metal ringing her neck, she pulled with all her might.

Spikes stabbed into her neck to deter her, but she bore the pain. The collar groaned, bent outwards, then cracked.

She grabbed the crack and tore it further, slipping her neck out from its angry grasp and bloody from puncture wounds.

The collar *clinked* the sidewalk where she left it.

3

SHE RAN — NOT KNOWING WHERE TO but only that it was away from the Kuro Mafia's building, and she didn't slow until her legs depleted of energy.

Buildings of glass and metal towered all around her into the sky like a forest she was now lost within. The night crowd and cars became background noise while she staggered into an alley beside a convenience store. She slid down behind a dumpster, pulled the hood of her jacket up and shivered, though it wasn't cold.

Questions floated around her: Where should she go? How could she make a living without her identity being found out?

A ramen shop. Yes, she could cook noodles, wear the cap over her bushy hair which would also conveniently

hide her ears. And no one would think twice about her fangs, thinking it a style choice—this was Japan, after all, home of the cosplayers. She'd find a quiet ramen shop to join at the next city over.

The pendant brushed against her chest and she touched it. If only she could unlock its secrets, find a portal leading to a world where she could live openly, freely…

Tack-tack.

She jerked in alarm and held her breath when a shadow extended into the alley, followed by bootsteps. Fists clenched, she crouched and readied to attack the shadow figure.

A cape swished, and she lunged out fist-first.

The man whirled and caught her fist in his hand, the force of her strength skidding his boots backwards across the pavement.

Streetlights reflected off the metal device against the side of his face.

"Toshi?" She yanked her hand free. Had he come to bring her back?

"I can't; you know I can't. Kuro wants me to sacrifice my life." She backed away. "You're an Altered. You understand, don't you? I need to escape."

Toshi's frown didn't change.

Panic rose in her throat. "You can escape with me! Two Altered stand a better chance than one. What's your opinion on ramen?"

"THERE IS NO ESCAPE."

"So, you want me to die?" She gazed up at him with the most pitiful doe eyes she could muster and waited.

His jaw twitched.

"I have a plan, a place to escape to," she said. Neither a solid plan, nor a solid place, but no need to discuss that right now!

She didn't want to fight Toshi; he looked tough for even a vempar to handle, and besides that, he was a fellow Altered. "Surely you don't want to spend the rest of your life serving the mafia, do you? Is that what your parents would've wanted for you?"

"DON'T TALK ABOUT MY PARENTS!"

Lotus shut her lips.

"THOSE WHO TRY TO ESCAPE ARE ALWAYS CAUGHT—AND ARE EXECUTED FOR IT. YOU WILL DIE. AND IF I LET YOU GO, I WILL DIE TOO."

Lotus reeled. This hauk guy was being impossible!

"You're not willing to take a chance at freedom? I'm telling you I have a plan! Living for Kuro isn't living, Toshi. We're already like dead people. But this is our one chance to *really* live! If you want to stay dead in the dark, then that's your choice, but don't force me to do the same with you."

Head high, Lotus brushed past him towards the mouth of the alley, fear in her gut, hoping he wouldn't grab her from behind and stop her.

"...ALREADY LIKE DEAD PEOPLE..."

She kept walking, and soon his steps followed her into the busy street.

"THE MAFIA WON'T STOP HUNTING YOU. NO ONE GETS AWAY. WHAT IS THIS GREAT PLAN YOU HAVE THAT MAKES YOU THINK YOU WILL SURVIVE?"·

Oh? Was he finally curious? She could be more persuasive than she thought.

"It's a bit long to explain, but once we reach a safe place where we can get some shuteye, I'll share the info." Hopefully adding "we" would draw him into the plan. "Make sure those Kuros aren't tracking you," she added.

Toshi didn't reply, but he did remove his watch and bury it in the soil of a flower planter.

The street became a bridge over Naka River, and Lotus continued to the city island on the other side, next crossing a smaller bridge off the island to reach the grand building she'd spotted with a sign on the front: Canal Metropolis.

Indeed, that's what it was. She'd always wanted to see this place, ever since an article listed it as one of the top places to shop in Japan. Made up of a series of canals weaving through glamorous, curvy buildings, the place was every bit a shopper's paradise—clothing stores, appliances, geeky tech, and restaurants—and also the perfect area to lay low for a while.

Lotus crossed one of the narrow canals, night waters lapping beneath the little stone bridge and glittering in the Metropolis lights. Reaching a second canal, she chose to follow its weaving path for a long ways and halted when a series of hedges and a food stall came into view.

Taking a seat behind the hedges, and savoring the sweet, salty aroma wafting from food being fried, Lotus tried to keep calm. Toshi was facing her with a look that needed no words to explain.

"Okay, we can talk now. But you must promise to keep what I'm about to tell you secret," she urged. "Don't go betraying me; agreed?"

"*THAT DEPENDS ON HOW PLAUSIBLE YOUR PLAN IS.*"

"Keep it secret, or I won't tell!"

"*FINE. BUT I'LL STILL HAUL YOU BACK TO KURO IF I DON'T ACCEPT YOUR PLAN.*"

Lotus wanted to smack that computer voice and his skeptical frown, but she refrained and fished the pendant out from beneath her shirt. "Have you ever heard the story of the Beorgan Society?"

Toshi shook his head, feathers at the nape of his neck swishing with the gesture.

"Okay, that'll make this harder to explain." She sucked in a breath. "The Beorgan Society was a group of genius Altered who worked together to find a place where our kind could live in peace. They discovered such a place via a portal which led them to another world. Most of our kind left Earth to go claim the new world, and the Society went with them, but not before leaving clues behind for those of us who chose to stay here. This pendant I have is a clue that leads to the portal. If we follow it, we can find the portal and leave this world. We can have a new life, in a *new* world! Can you imagine what that would be like? No more worries, no more fear of humans taking you captive. We'd be free!" Exuberance filled her just thinking of it.

Toshi's long stare didn't blink. He slowly reached a gloved hand and gripped the top of her hair, shaking her head back and forth.

"Knock it off!" She yanked at his arm. He released her and sat back, still staring.

"A SHAKE MAY FIX A WONKY COMPUTER, BUT IT CAN'T FIX A FLESHY BRAIN, CAN IT?"

Lotus puffed out her cheeks. "I'm not wonky in the head! The story's true, and I'm going to find that portal! So, you can either tag along and find freedom with me, or brood in this miserable place."

"WHERE IS THE CLUE?"

She hesitated, crossed her arms. "I'm still working on that."

"YOU DON'T HAVE A MAP?"

She avoided his gaze.

"WHAT SORT OF PLAN DOESN'T HAVE A MAP?" He grabbed her arm. *"THIS IS POINTLESS, AND YOU'RE*

WASTING MY TIME. I WAS FOOLISH TO GIVE YOU A CHANCE."

"But it's the truth! This pendant does have a map. I just need more time to find it—"

"TIME IS UP." Toshi yanked her to her feet.

Lotus fell forward, bumping into him, and seized the chance to twist free and duck behind him: delivering a kick to his back that sent him sprawling into the canal.

She ran as the water made a large splash, and in her haste surprised several shoppers who quickly scurried out of her way.

Curved buildings and weaving pathways of water passed by, and she didn't slow until Canal Metropolis came to an end and mixed with the regular city buildings surrounding it. The familiar ruckus of cars and people and strange smells met her senses.

There was a heavy amount of men walking the streets here, some in suits, most in leather and sporting wild, colorful hair. One with spiked hair pointed at her and said something to his friends.

She edged away quickly.

A bright pink neon sign of a cat lady to her left made her realize she'd stumbled into a red-light district. Panicking inwardly, she quickened her pace and kept the hood of her jacket up.

Her legs were like jelly. She'd never walked so much in her life! Well, except for her life before, on the farm; it felt so distant and unreal.

Lotus finally reached the next district, and the unsavory crowd fizzled into a regular night crowd of late shoppers and video gamers heading into gaming buildings.

Lotus slid into a tiny alley and used her vempar strength to jump. She just barely grabbed the edge of a low dipping roof and hoisted herself up onto it. She rested on the corner eave, the bumpy Asian roof tiles digging into her backside.

Large drones transporting packages soared the sky of the city above her, their little lights blinking against morbid clouds. She watched them as she let her racing heartbeat slow.

The giant screen of a building across the square from her played a news channel, and she eyed it for a while. Images of warships, missile preparations, and angry politicians flashed behind the news reporter. Headlines rolled by: A New World War Soon To Be A Reality, Long-Standing Truces Shattered, and then something about Major Earthquakes On The Rise: Changing Landscapes Across The Globe, and other disasters she didn't bother reading.

Lotus shut her eyes. She couldn't afford to care what went on in the world right now, except to care that she must escape it. Working at a ramen shop could never be enough.

Her fingers clenched the pendant, its one bumpy side digging in her thumb. "Show me the way, won't you? The world's about to end. I don't want to end with it."

What was that bumpy side? Lotus tried looking, but it was too dark to see clearly.

Why couldn't Toshi understand? It would've been nice to have a companion in this.

She scooted up to a leveler part of the roof and curled into a ball. Her body groaned; there would be no life-energy meal tonight, let alone food for her stomach.

Exhaustion sapped at her until she fell asleep.

4

A BRIGHTNESS INTERRUPTED HER SLEEP, glowing white behind her eyelids to the point that Lotus couldn't ignore it any longer.

She groaned and sat up, and the moment she opened her eyes she had to squint and shield with a hand.

The world was enveloped in light. Daylight. A bright thing called the sun replacing streetlights and bulbs.

"*Aagh.*" She blinked repeatedly. She shimmied down off the roof, landing her sneakers in the still-dark alley. How many years had it been since she'd last been out during the day?

She peeked out the alley and into the open square beyond buzzing with people of the work and daytime crowd.

After her eyes adjusted some, Lotus joined the crowd and kept a look out for any darkly clad figures.

She read the signs of passing stores along the way — luxury tech, anime otaku, shoe ware, antiques. She halted at the last one, eyeing a certain object there in the window display.

Lotus entered the shop, which was fashioned to look like an antique itself: old wood and bamboo ceiling and floors. She smiled to the owner, who narrowed his creased gaze in return, and made her way over to the display. She lingered until she was sure no one was watching, then snatched the magnifying glass from behind the window and shuffled backwards to stand behind a row of old baskets.

She held the bumpy side of the crystal pendant up to the magnifying glass.

The bump didn't seem to be anything much, but the feel of it had to mean *something*. She drifted her thumb up from the bump toward the metal leaves and pushed up against them.

Something snapped.

For a moment she feared her strength had broken a leaf. But then the head of leaves lifted, and the crystal pendant fell open into two joined halves.

She gave a start. The leaves were a clasp that held the halves closed!

She ran the magnifying glass across the inside halves of the crystal eagerly, and there found a shape: something not quite a circle and looking as if it'd been etched there on purpose, with dips and bends and a jagged coastline.

Coastline? It resembled an island.

And just north of it sat three tiny bumps; one on the very left had a strange etched X.

"Is this…a map?" Lotus covered her mouth, hoping no one had overhead.

If it *was* a map, it was sorely lacking in detail and

directions and names. How was she supposed to know what island this was? Japan was full of islands!

"Oh well. Can't let that stop me." Thrill danced through her. The map, she'd finally found it! It really was inside the necklace, all along!

Dad would have been elated, gotten out his fiddle and played a jig. How she wished she could show him, share in this moment.

She fished for cash and bought the magnifying glass. She also bought a blue knit cap at the next store over to cover her ears and diminish the brightness of her orange hair—wearing a hood all the time was too suspicious.

Mou, she was tired and starving! Her leftover change wasn't enough to buy a full meal, so she settled for melon bread from a bakery. As she walked on, and stuffed the last piece into her mouth, a hand grabbed her arm.

She yelped as it pulled her sideways into a gap between buildings. She threw her fist, and a gloved hand caught it, same as last time.

"Darn it, how do you keep finding me?"

"IT'S MY JOB, AND YOU'RE TOO EASY TO SPOT." Toshi's grip was like iron, and in the weakened state she was in she couldn't fight much.

"I found the map!" she shouted before he could cuff her hands. She lowered her voice. "It's very tiny, but it's there. We can leave this world!"

Toshi's gaze remained hardened, and his clothes looked damp.

"I'm not trying to trick you, honest. Just let me show you." Lotus waited as he regarded her for a moment, then he released his grip on her wrists and shifted to block her from the alley mouth and any chance at escape.

Lotus took out the magnifying glass and showed him the pendant through it. "This is the outline of an island, here in Japan. See this X marking? That's got to be where the portal is." She inched nearer, tipping her head to look him in the eye. "Haven't you ever wanted to be free of humans? Free of being used by them, free to soar the skies on your wings?"

Something flashed across Toshi's green gaze at her words. She paused, holding her breath. He took the magnifying glass and leaned close, peering at the pendant now dangling open.

Seconds ticked by. He straightened, dropping the glass into her jacket pocket. *"IF YOU CAN PROVE THIS ISLAND IS REAL, THEN I WILL CONSIDER ASSISTING YOU."*

"Deal!" Lotus grinned, and grabbing his gloved hand pulled him out into the street. "All we need is a big ol' map of Japan, now. Where should we look?" Unfortunately, she'd left her miPod back in her jail room.

Toshi raised his arm to point at a shop: a computer café. "Ah, perfect! Um, do you have any cash?" You couldn't use their computers for free.

He nodded and started for the shop, pulling her forward by the wrist.

She trotted to keep up and tried to act natural. "Don't grip me like I'm a prisoner—you'll draw attention!" she hissed.

He slowed his pace but didn't release her until they entered the glass door. He handed her cash; she frowned, taking it and stomping up to the counter to buy computer time and a coffee. Toshi wasn't taking any chances that she might escape, letting her do the work so he could keep his eyes glued to her back and block the exist.

Once Lotus got her mug of bitter coffee, she found their designated computer; Toshi took the chair beside hers. It took a while for the device to turn on and then get to the internet's loaded files of Japan maps.

She squinted at the list of images that came up. Toshi leaned close to her shoulder, inspecting them. His finger tapped on one of the map images, opening it before she could choose one herself. She bit her tongue, halting the remark she wanted to make.

The opened map image was detailed. She tried to recall the shape of the island on the crystal while scanning the numerous clusters of land dotting Japan's coastline. Toshi touched the air screen again, using two fingers to zoom in on smaller islands.

Time passed, and the line of Toshi's mouth thinned further and further. Worry teased the back of Lotus's mind, and she analyzed the pendant one more time.

They scanned the south-western end of Japan and zoomed in. "Wait!" Lotus jabbed at the screen, and the view finder zoomed in on a dot of northern Nagasaki Prefecture. The dot was an island with a curious, rugged outline and miniature islands along its coast. "Iki Island…this has to be it!"

She peered at the crystal through the magnifying glass once more to be sure, and Toshi bent over her shoulder to check. "Don't you think?" she asked him, slightly leaning since he was so close.

His gaze roved over the map before he nodded.

Relief flooded through her. "We'd better get this printed." She clicked on the Print icon. A sudden wave of dizziness made her shut her eyes and rub her forehead.

Toshi tugged her jacket sleeve and pointed at the door. She frowned with a question, until he stood and motioned for her to follow him outside. She did, map in hand, reluctant to leave the café's air-conditioning.

Out on the sidewalk, Toshi grabbed her hand, pulling her along as he made his way through the crowd, breaking right and into a small park and benches. He had her sit.

"HAVE YOU CONSUMED ANY LIFE-ENERGY?"

It dawned on her that he hadn't been speaking in the café or in closed spaces where his computer voice might draw attention. The park was roomy, and people who sat on the other benches either wore earphones or were busy discussing dating advice.

Lotus shook her head. Toshi rolled back the black sleeve of his dust jacket, exposing his arm but leaving his glove on.

He held his arm out to her, and it took her a moment to understand.

"No, Toshi, I can't! I've never taken any from a person before. I grew up on animals, and they always died."

Toshi didn't move. She turned her face away.

"VEMPARS ARE NOT MEANT TO LIVE ON THE LIFE-ENERGY OF ANIMALS. IT CAN MAKE THEM ILL AND WEAK."

Lotus thought back to the sick feeling she got whenever she absorbed the energy of an animal, how she wanted to vomit, and how sickly her parents used to always seem.

She chewed her lip. Toshi brought his arm closer.

Maybe…he was right.

She reached to touch his bare skin. Eyes closed, she felt through the palm of her hand and into his skin, seeking out the core of life-energy that filled every being. The receptors in her palm drew the found energy into her hand, through her arm to her core—replenishing the life-energy which her body could not create.

She wasn't sure how much to take and stopped. Her headache fled. "Thank you," she told him.

He nodded. His cheeks were paler, but there was no other indication that he'd been harmed.

Why didn't he just take the pendant and leave her there, instead of helping her regain her strength? She wondered.

Maybe he wasn't all that bad?

"We should plan our route," she said, tearing her gaze away.

"THE NEAREST ROUTE TO IKI IS THROUGH HAKATA PORT. THERE'S A FERRY THAT GOES DIRECTLY TO THE ISLAND."

Lotus didn't have a pen but used a dirt smudge to mark the port on the printed map. "Northward to the port we go, then, travel buddy." She stood and clapped his shoulder. He shrugged her hand off.

"IF THERE IS NO PORTAL, I'M TAKING YOU BACK TO KURO."

"We'll find it, don't worry!" she fake-laughed it off. "How long do you think we have before Kuro gets suspicious and sends someone else to find me?"

Toshi glanced to the sky. *"HOURS. I HAVE NOT REPORTED BACK SINCE LAST NIGHT."*

"Yikes. Let's get a move on."

The streets were more crowded than ever, now; Lotus pushed and shoved her way through, and Toshi trailed behind. She finally saw the reason *why* when their street crossed into an open square:

A vehicle the size of a truck bore a green puppet dragon's head at the front and a tail at the back, and it made its way down the street around the square, dragon jaws opening and closing. Music of bells, pots and pans filled the air with rhythm. A group of children and young ladies waved pink and red fans as they danced in a pattern, dressed in pinks and grays, following the dragon. Paper lanterns with inked writing swayed on poles carried by men.

Lotus backed up with the onlookers to watch and make room; some of the crowd were wearing masks and festive garments and cheered.

"THE HAKATA DONTAKU FESTIVAL," said Toshi.

She'd never seen a festival, not in a city like this. Colors were everywhere, more colors than she knew existed in real life. An army of women in flowery kimonos and wide pink hats marched down the festival path, waving and fluttering more elaborate fans than the previous younger group.

After them trotted a man on a horse, his face an evil black mask, and a host of traditionally dressed men encircled him. Chimes and music filled the air as more groups came, some from schools and others from bands.

Toshi nudged her shoulder. She pulled her attention away from the wondrous sight and continued through the sea of pedestrians, who now stood in place to watch.

Men dressed in red robes and creepy monkey-like masks danced past, if you could call the strange movements dancing. Horns beeped, and she craned her neck to see a stream of trucks decked out in bright paints, light bulbs, and fantastic designs. She didn't have much time to decipher them as she shoved through the crowd and into a less busy alley.

It was going to be a long walk to reach Hakata Port through the festivities.

After several hours, her stomach was growling. Toshi glanced at her. She blushed, pouted, and looked away.

"WAIT HERE," he said, motioning to a bench. Too tired to care, she sat and watched as he slipped through the crowd to a cluster of food stalls set out specially for the festival. He returned like a silent wraith and held out to her a boat of fried *takoyaki*. She gratefully munched the dumpling-shaped food, filled with diced octopus and slathered in a salty sweet brown sauce.

She paused long enough to offer him some; he only took a few.

More clamoring pots and chimes moved past as they ate; seated, she couldn't see above the crowd's heads.

"I'm going to the restroom," she told Toshi before rising and scanning the area. There was a fast-food restaurant at a street corner, and she headed toward it. In the crowd stood a masked man: a hideous face of gray skin, lower jaw teeth that jutted up like tusks, and something like horns poking out from wild hair.

An image flashed in Lotus's mind of the old farmhouse: her dad by the door, a spear running through his chest. She shuddered and reached the fast-food place, going inside to the restrooms.

Her hands trembled as she washed them in the sink. It would all be over soon, once they reached Iki and found the portal. She had to remember that. Her parents' sacrifice would not be in vain.

Stepping back outside, she leaned against the wall and took out the map, cementing the pattern in her mind to busy herself.

Dad's face flashed by, his smile, the rug they used to sit on as he told her stories of mythical creatures, and the moments when they all sat on the porch to watch the sunset…before guns and blood put an end to everything.

Lotus tried to focus on the map and still her hands.

She glanced up, and the gray hideous mask appeared a step away from her, turned facing her.

She froze. The man's hand lifted the mask off: beneath it the same tusked face as the mask, and a fleshy mouth which grinned at her.

A startled gasp caught in her throat, and his gray hand tore the map from her grasp before she could turn and run. "Kuro wants to see you."

The huge trollic—exactly like the one who had killed Dad—grabbed for her.

5

LOTUS DARTED THROUGH THE CROWD—evading the trollic and letting the bustle of people slow him down—desperate to find the bench and Toshi. Heavy boots pursued her.

She spotted the bench. "Toshi!" But the hauk guy was no longer there.

She paused, looking around, dazed like a deer in the headlights.

The trollic shoved three people aside as he reached the bench, and Lotus moved to keep the bench between them, glancing about for a path of escape. A cloak flapped around the trollic, and beneath it she caught a glimpse of weapons, gear, and armor plates strapped around muscles—this was a bounty hunter, no ordinary trollic.

The hunter's tusked jaws grinned, and he pulled out a stocky gun, its barrel full of attached ropes—like the ropes that had captured her all those years ago.

As he took aim, she readied to run, knowing she wouldn't get far if he was a good shot.

Thmp!

A kick caught the Trollic's arm, sending him skidding backwards, as Toshi descended through the air, leg first, a wing like that of a hawk propelling him and adding to the force of the impact, feathers at the back of his calves and elbows also fanned out.

Lotus, so stunned when he landed, didn't feel Toshi grab her hand and pull her away into the streets.

She ran mechanically, Toshi leading them down path after concrete path, crossing through parades and dances, earning shouts of anger, then across a bridge and down a side alley. He dove through an unlocked cellar door. There, they stopped and panted.

Lotus couldn't form the words, but Toshi must have understood. "*TROLLIC TRACKER. HE'S AN INFAMOUS BOUNTY HUNTER,*" he breathed as the device in his ears spoke for him. "*KURO HIRED THE BEST...AND NOW HE KNOWS I'M WITH YOU. I WON'T BE ABLE TO GO BACK.*" He said it like he hadn't fully realized until now what he'd been doing, like he'd just lost something important.

"The mafia wasn't your home, Toshi, just like it wasn't mine," Lotus finally said. "I don't regret leaving. We're going to find a better place than this, remember?"

He glanced at her, then looked at the shabby door, grim. "*DID HE SEE THE MAP?*"

She was about to say no when she remembered. "He ripped it from my hands before I realized what was happening...I'm sorry."

"WE CAN NO LONGER GO TO HAKATA PORT. WE MUST TAKE THE TRAIN AND FIND A DIFFERENT PORT FARTHER AWAY."

"No plane rides?"

"KURO WILL HAVE WATCHDOGS AT EVERY AIRPORT, BY NOW. IT IS THE FIRST THING HE WILL EXPECT US TO DO."

She wanted to say more, ask more, but Toshi exited the cellar and motioned her along. It took an hour of weaving through streets and shadows and parade crowds before Hakata Station's glass and metal building reared its head. Large letters spelling JR Hakata City arched over the glass foyer entrance.

Toshi's vigilant gaze continued to scan left and right and every shadow they neared, putting Lotus's nerves further on edge. They crossed a broad, tiled corridor with the smoothest floor and brightest lights she'd ever seen. Glass panels rose throughout the space like columns: displaying the latest footwear, perfume, and other tempting items.

Chatter and the smells of fast-food being cooked filled the station while she followed Toshi. She marveled at corridors lined with shops and a glass roof skylight letting in the sun. The hauk made a straight line for the wall of maps, and there muttered to himself as he plotted a course he didn't bother sharing aloud. Lotus sunk her chin below her shoulders, guessing he wasn't going to trust her with information anymore after her mishap.

Toshi went over to one of the large machines she'd seen people punching buttons on, and he pressed buttons while the machine's voice asked him questions. He slipped cash into a slot, and the machine popped out two tickets, one which he handed her.

He went over to a different row of machines, through which people were filing and inserting their tickets. She did as he did, giving and taking her ticket from the machine and walking through the narrow space to get to the other side. She followed him up a flight of stairs opening onto a platform outdoors, train tracks running on either side.

She knew what trains looked like from the internet, but like so many things, had never seen one in real life. She stood next to him a few feet away from the platform's edge, standing and saying nothing, Toshi continuing to scan the area, turning his head about.

Lotus's attention shifted to the bustle of people about the platforms. A little girl with dark hair trailed after her parents, pulling along behind her a pink suitcase on wheels and her other arm hugging a Sailor Moon doll to her chest.

The floor rumbled under their shoes, and a loud screeching and whine hurt her ears as a train came in off to her right. It came gliding down a rail line through the sky, the train along it slowing to land upon the tracks in the ground. The long vehicle made of attached train cars squealed and made a puffing sound when it finally came to a stop, and a row of doors hissed open.

Toshi's hand on her back pushed her into the train car with him. The bench seats were orange, plush, and new along both walls, and she quickly took a spot by a window. Toshi sat at the end of the bench, leaving a gap between them.

She thinned her lips. "Can't stand to sit that close to me?"

He looked at her puzzled, then went back to scanning their train car as more people poured in. Maybe he had some other reason for taking the seat closest to the doors. And he wasn't going to risk drawing attention by speaking to her—must be hard having a computer for a voice.

The train began puffing and squealing once more, and

carried their car forward, soon rising off the ground and running along the rail line course through the air.

She watched the platform and people shrink as the train moved faster and faster; buildings and cars whipped past. The sky was blue—the blue she used to remember—with scattered lumpy clouds along the eastern horizon.

Lotus settled back to relax and watch the scenery shift by. Her back and shoulders were stiff from the unceasing tension of last night. A baby cried while the mother tried rocking him to sleep, the train hummed, and a group to the back left kept bickering. Lotus soon wished she had her miPod to drown it all out.

Beyond the window, they crossed a wide river. Canoe-like boats bobbed, some strung with unlit red paper lanterns. Larger boats were decked out with festive décor similar to the parade trucks. More buildings passed. The patches of greenery that were parks caught her eye: green reminders that called up images of the rice paddies and bamboo woods.

She met Toshi's gaze briefly, though he didn't seem to see her. There wasn't a reason to be tense while they were flying through the city, was there? No enemy could board the train, now.

Well, if he wanted to stay alert, that was fine. But she needed rest.

A dark bird zipped past the window, and Toshi's head whipped toward the glass.

Lotus sent him a questioning look, which was meant to warn him to cool down and act more normal. That is, before a high whirring sound that reminded her of dentists stung her ears. What *was* that?

Toshi's gaze shot up to the metal roof.

"GO."

When she didn't move, he pulled her up by the arm and motioned to the train car in front of theirs. The whirring sound changed into orange sparks, and a spinning saw emerged cutting through the car's roof.

Other people saw it and began shouting. The baby wailed. The bickering group fell silent.

A slab of metal roof peeled back and the trollic's demonish face filled the gap, looking straight at Lotus and chuckling around his yellowed tusks.

Lotus bolted for the door that connected their train car to the next, and the trollic's heavy leather boots came through the roof as the beast dropped into the car.

Toshi leaped up, drawing twin guns he'd had hidden, and fired.

The blasts made Trollic Tracker slide back, the bullets bouncing off his armor, and he raised his arm: firing bullets from a barrel belted to his forearm.

Toshi ducked left and right, but there wasn't much room.

Lotus entered the next car and turned, watching. People were lying flat on the floor and crawling under the seats to avoid the shots. If Trollic kept shooting, not only Toshi but others would get injured or worse.

Lotus gathered strength into her legs and into her fist. In one leap she shot up to the ceiling and with her fist punched through the metal. She fell back down and leaped again: soaring through the new ceiling gap and out into the sky.

Trollic saw her disappear, holstered his gun, and leaped through the ceiling gap he'd cut.

Lotus landed unsteadily on a train car and waved her arms to steady herself against the air rushing past with the train's momentum.

Trollic landed two cars down from her, wild hair whipping. "Guns won't work as well on you. Cut off the head, or cut out the heart, like I did your father—that's the way to do it." His meaty hand reached behind his back, pulling free a katana blade.

He really *was* the one who'd killed her dad, her mom, destroyed her life. Emotions rattled through her bones and kept her from moving as Trollic stepped across the cars between them.

'*Move!*' she told her body.

One car stood between them. Half a car stood between them. She couldn't unfreeze.

The katana sword rose, the sharp edge tilted.

Lotus raised her arms in defense.

The katana came down, and something blocked her sight.

She peered between her raised arms to see Toshi's back. He held both his guns up, blades thrust out from slots beside the barrels, gun handles clicked back to be held like sword hilts. He blocked the katana's stroke with both blades crossed.

Trollic loomed taller, his strength greater. Toshi shoved his crossed blades and kicked Trollic's lower stomach at the same time, unbalancing him enough for Toshi to turn and grab her and hurry across the train cars.

Toshi halted abruptly, and she stumbled. His arms wrapped around her waist so suddenly that she yelped. "*HOLD ON TO ME. TIGHTLY.*"

"What are you do—?" Lotus didn't get a chance to ask; he leaned forward over the edge of the train.

She gripped her arms around him and held on tight as they fell off, plummeting through the air.

Buildings and a broad park grew below them. She tried to scream but the wind stole the breath from her lungs. She could only see sky as Toshi turned her back to face the approaching ground.

Then Toshi's wing spread out like a hang glider.

The wind tore at his feathers, shaking his wing. She could feel him working to stabilize their descent, but without two wings they were unbalanced. The feathers sticking out of slots in his clothes at his calves and elbows spread out like small fans, and he curled his large wing to cup an updraft.

The air held under his wing, and their fall slowed…until they landed in a stand of leaves and branches.

Lotus tumbled ungracefully out of a tree to the ground.

Scratched and bruised, she rolled over to right herself and sat up, pulling twigs out of her mangled curls, and feeling a cracked rib Healing.

A hand on her shoulder made her jump. It was Toshi, his face close, crouched behind her shoulder. He indicated upwards with his gaze; she followed and saw a dark figure gliding through the sky: Trollic Tracker.

She hurried after Toshi, leaving where they'd landed, and headed deeper into the park.

Rising police sirens fueled her panic—they'd be after the three suspects involved in a shoot-out on a public train.

Cherry blossoms painted the trees, and their sweet scent had filled the park. Lotus breathed it in. Slanted walls of stone and castle shapes rose around them from the grass—ancient and laced in moss. They used the walls and uneven ground to keep out of sight and moved farther and farther away from where Trollic had seen them land.

They paused at a wall's corner, the soft moss growing on it brushed her hand. Toshi held his left side for a moment.

Stopped now, she had time to see his wing folded at an odd angle out from his cape, and the way he was limping and bent forward. Shot at in a confined train car, he couldn't have gotten out of there unscathed.

"You need Healing," she said at his back. But he shook his head and rounded the corner, hurrying through a narrow pass between two steeply slanted walls. Pink petals floated down from a breeze to litter the green.

Lotus gritted her teeth, chasing after him. Then her foot got stuck. "*Aak.*"

She yanked her ankle free, only for her other foot to sink into the ground. "What the?"

Toshi halted, came back, keeping one eye to the sky.

"I'm sinking into the ground—" The moment she said it, the ground opened beneath them and they fell through into darkness.

Lotus landed on hard dirt and groaned, blinking to see, and rubbing her backside. A dim spot of light came in from where they'd fallen, and she could make out part of a stone wall and the rest walls of dirt. "What did we fall into?"

Toshi made a sound, something like a pained groan, and worked to sit himself up and prop his back against the mildew stone. He was breathing hard and sweating. She moved to his side and saw blood.

"I doubt that bounty hunter will find us here. We have time, so I'm going to have to take some of your clothes off," Lotus told him.

He gave her a look, and she rolled her eyes. "Don't worry, it's just for Healing. I won't let myself be tempted by your impeccably attractive muscles," she said with sarcasm.

She pulled the dust jacket back and let him slip his arms free, then carefully lifted his shirt off. Blood trickled from two bullet wounds, and bruises made wide patches of purple skin.

She sucked in a breath. This was going to take a while.

The bullets lay in the dirt as Lotus finished Healing. "Let me have a look at your wing."

Toshi didn't budge, keeping his back to the wall. "You probably sprained it. Let me see." She shoved at his shoulder, trying to turn him, and he refused to move, fixing his glare on her. "I know you've only got one wing. There's nothing to be ashamed of. Now, move!"

Toshi set his jaw firmly.

"Fine! Go ahead and suffer." Lotus gave up and sat back.

They stayed silent for a while.

"HOW DO YOU KNOW THERE'S REALLY A PORTAL WAITING THERE? THAT THIS ANCIENT TALE IS REAL? WHAT IF, AFTER ALL YOU GO THROUGH TO REACH IKI ISLAND, NOTHING IS THERE? IT WOULD ALL HAVE BEEN A WASTE, AND YOU'LL BE CAUGHT BY KURO."

Lotus shifted to look at him. He faced forward, charcoal hair with white streaks falling about his sweaty cheeks and angling out with feathers from the back. He'd lost his place in the mafia, just as she had, but it had been her choice to make.

"We can't know unless we try, Toshi. Even if it means the end for me, if it's the direction God is pointing me towards, then it's worth a try. Don't you think?"

"YOU COULD TRY TO FLEE JAPAN, GO SOMEWHERE ELSE KURO WON'T FIND YOU."

"And give up this chance at a new world?"

He turned his head away. *"YOU HAVE TOO MUCH FAITH."*

"And you have too little. I can guess you've had a hard life, but that's why you need faith all the more."

Toshi drew his knees up, his hands rested on the tops of his thick, leather boots. *"YOU THINK THAT BECAUSE YOU'VE SUFFERED FOR PART OF YOUR LIFE,*

YOU UNDERSTAND WHAT IT'S LIKE TO BE ME? YOU DON'T KNOW ANYTHING. YOU'VE NEVER HAD TO FIGHT TO SURVIVE EVERY DAY, AND HOPE YOU REMAIN USEFUL TO SOMEONE SO YOU DON'T END UP DEAD. YOU LIVED ON A PERFECT RICE FARM, AND KURO'S SAFE CELL AFTER THAT."

"Hey, just because I didn't live your life doesn't mean I didn't suffer and feel pain and want it all to end. Don't act like I didn't go through anything!" Lotus clenched her fingers. "Sure, I was safe as Kuro's money-making slave, but I was still a slave. Forced to Heal wicked people I knew the world would be better off without, forced to stay in the dark underground away from daylight, away from fresh air and real people to talk to. And always remembering that it was *my* fault I wanted to see the circus that day, *my* fault that my parents were found and murdered...*my* fault. Does Kuro have some file or something on me that you read?"

"*YES.*" Toshi's chin turned down to his chest. He shifted onto his knees and crouched down on his stomach so that his wing showed.

Lotus took the gesture as permission, and ran her hands along the feathers, unfolding the wing. She focused on Healing the sprained muscle and damaged feathers, and took note of the stub of bone that was all there was left of the missing wing. The stub was a straight line, hacked by a blade. She felt the urge to ask but held her tongue.

Her thoughts wandered while she worked, and a young boy with wings flew into her memory: thrill on his face as he soared high above the circus crowd, fearless as he dove through hoops of fire that singed the tips of his wings. He lived to fly, the sky his home, and to come back down at the end of the show was like coming back down to a prison.

Could this same person be...?

Finished, a wave of weariness came over her and she leaned back, let her eyes close. When she opened them again, it was dark beyond the cave-in hole.

6

"Oh wow, I didn't mean to fall asleep." Lotus rubbed her eyelids. No more police sirens could be heard; they must have moved their search elsewhere.

Toshi blinked awake and shifted to put his shirt back on. "Feel better?"

He nodded and glanced her way briefly. "*THANK YOU.*"

She paused, surprised for a second. "Sure thing."

"*DO YOU NEED LIFE-ENERGY?*"

After Healing both him and herself, she did. Her stomach growled, too. Toshi held out his arm. "No, not from you. I need you to be at your strongest."

He retracted his arm and stood to peer up at the cave-in opening.

After a while, he deemed it safe enough and jumped up, gripping the grassy edge, pulling himself out of the underground chamber.

Lotus called after him quietly, but he had vanished.

She waited. And waited. Until nerves got the better of her, and she bunched her muscles and leaped clumsily out of the grassy hole. She landed against a slanted stone wall and rested on her hand; she inhaled the sweetened cool air. The cherry blossoms were vaguely visible in the surrounding city light. The eastern sky—what bits she could see of it—was just starting to gray, signaling the approach of dawn.

A thump to her left made her jump. A suited man appeared unconscious on the ground, and standing over him: Toshi. He pointed to the man.

"You just—? No, Toshi, I can't just take some random human's life-energy!"

"WHY NOT? YOU'LL DIE WITHOUT IT. AND IT'S NOT LIKE THE HUMAN WON'T RECOVER LATER."

She frowned that he could so easily grab someone off the street, knock them out, and think there was nothing wrong with that. But she *would* get weak and die, so she rested her palm against the human's bare neck and absorbed only the amount she needed.

A black wig and a new jacket landed in front of her. She blinked at the random items.

"WEAR THESE."

Toshi was putting on a brown wig, and the man's fedora hat and coat. She didn't dare to ask how he'd gotten the items as she put on the disguise.

Toshi motioned her to follow, and they made their way through the park, drawing closer to three towering blue buildings.

The park ended at a wide street which they hurried across.

They ducked under a bus stop awning. "What are we doing?" she asked him, and he pointed to the English word "bus" on a flyer on the glass back wall. She peered out into the night, wondering where Trollic Tracker could be hiding from the police and waiting for them. It was risky standing here, but it could also mean them getting out of the city faster.

It wasn't a long wait before a large white-and-blue bus pulled up to a huffing-puffing stop. Toshi told the driver, *"TWO FOR MEINOHAMA STATION."*

The bus driver regarded the device looped around the back of his head attached in each ear, and then her with stray orange hair strands peeking from under the black wig.

The driver muttered something and let them on.

Once they took their seats, she murmured, "Good thing this land is full of cosplayers, or we'd really stand out."

She could've sworn Toshi's lips twitched in a brief smile, though his posture remained vigilant and stoic.

Lotus tried to get comfortable despite the seat's missing chunks of fabric and watched the city lights and life rush by the scratched window as the bus wheeled forward. She thought about napping, but each jolt and turn of the bus snapped her alert, making her imagine the hideous beast coming through the ceiling again.

Soon, the bus puffed to a stop, and Toshi tapped her arm.

They got off, stepping into the parking lot of Meinohama Station, which softly glowed. Blue sculptures like waves rose to her right. She trotted behind Toshi and into the train station. It wasn't as grand as Hakata, and they were faster getting to the train platform.

Pairs of police officers roamed the halls, no doubt looking for *them* and Trollic. Lotus rubbed her rumbling stomach.

The train arrived, brakes squealing as the first had, only this train's tracks followed the ground instead of running through the air—an older, traditional train. She took a seat on the bench, while Toshi remained standing.

Dawn blossomed beyond the window, silhouetting a blanket of clouds that resembled bubble foam. She scratched under the wig.

Cars, bustling streets, and buildings blurred as she thought about Trollic, the way her legs wouldn't move when he came at her. She couldn't be like that; she couldn't let fear freeze her again.

The land melted into blue, and sand and rocks ran off into an ocean, endless waves lapping on and on until they met with the horizon and there kissed the sky. She stared in awe unashamedly and heard what might have been a chuckle.

The ocean—her first, real view of the ocean. It was glorious.

The scenery was swallowed up as the train departed from the coastline to cross country and cut through the next big city. A billboard reading Itoshima City streaked past. The soaring and curved skyscrapers made the cityscape resemble something from science fiction.

The train slowed into a station, picking up and relinquishing passengers. She studied those who boarded, mostly of the working crowd. A large Japanese man took up a lot of space, and she nearly bolted thinking it was Trollic, but the man's fleshy face was pudgy and human.

The train huffed along the tracks once again. She could smell sauced meat and rice from someone's bento lunch, and her stomach ached more. Three girls in the back bench were dressed like Naruto characters and giggling, on their way to some cosplay event. Several Asians glanced at Toshi's brown skin; one of them sent him a flirty wink, which he failed to notice.

Lotus rolled her eyes and focused back on the passing scenery of buildings and a swarm of delivery drones taking flight into the morning.

She itched at the wig—why did this one have to be so darn uncomfortable?

A sudden loud sound jolted the train cars and she bounced in her seat.

The three girls screamed. People ducked their heads, staring all about in a panic, or bolted to their feet to run for the exits. Toshi pushed his way to the boarding door to see out.

She could smell smoke. She shared a look with Toshi across the space and didn't need to be told what it was.

The train car behind them shook with a boom.

Screams rent the air, and police from the front car rushed in, guns drawn. Toshi kept the brim of his fedora down as the crowd tried to get out of the officers' way.

Through the window in the door to the car behind them, smoke could be seen. One officer opened the door—to step through and check on the passengers there—and a large, clawed hand grabbed his arm, pulling him into the smoke screen.

Gun shots sounded.

The officers in their car shouted and readied to shoot; the passengers huddled and whimpered, pressing themselves to the walls and as far from gunfire as possible.

A wide cylinder poked through the smoke: the tip of a big gun.

"Get down!" Lotus shouted.

Toshi slammed the emergency button, opening the car's side door.

Gunfire rang. Passengers ducked against one another; police fell back wounded.

Trollic Tracker stepped through the writhing smoke.

Toshi's arm wrapped around Lotus and pulled her with him out the open side door.

They hit dirt and rolled, the momentum carrying their bodies down a slope leading from the train tracks. Their roll didn't stop until they met concrete.

Dizzy, Lotus made herself get up, scrapes all over her Healing. There was a buzzing all around them—the propellers of numerous drones lifting deliveries to travel across the sky.

They'd landed on a business's drone take-off platform.

Large boots thumped the ground as Trollic Tracker landed nearby.

"Toshi, hurry!" She waved him over to her before he could take out his guns, his fedora lost. She hopped onto the flat bed of a drone carrying stacks of thick boxes, which smelled of food.

The drone began its lift-off, and Toshi jumped on beside her.

"We'll have to knock off a few boxes for our weight. Sorry, whoever ordered all this!" With her foot she shoved off two boxes—thudding to the concrete—and the drone rose higher, faster.

She dared a glance down as the platform and everything else shrank, carried high by little more than a woven metal bed on whirring propellers. She sat, dizzy yet exhilarated to be doing such crazy things; she'd always wanted to ride on a drone!

Several drones broke off from the swarm to sail across to different parts of the city, while theirs and a few others headed south-west along the train's course.

A hum different from that of the propellers made Lotus look about in alarm.

Trollic's armored, hulking figure rose after them via jetpack, and he aimed his big gun: their drone the target.

It would be a long drop if they lost the drone, one she doubted Toshi could handle.

Toshi had his twin guns ready before she could warn him. *Blam-blam!*

Trollic had to dodge right and give up the shot. He rose and dipped to avoid Toshi's aim, while adjusting his own.

Toshi ducked behind the wall of stacked boxes as bullets sought him, some making holes in the board. He fired back, peeking his head out just enough to aim.

Lotus hid behind the stacks, pondering what to do. Trollic continued swerving left and right, then blasted a hole through the box nearest Toshi's head. Toshi flattened to the metal drone bed and continued firing. In a drawn-out fight, Lotus knew Trollic Tracker was more equipped. She ripped open one of the boxes and began digging through it.

She heard a sound: the kind that fine blades make when cutting through the air, and raised her head to look, only to quickly duck back down.

Sharp shurikens—metal blades in the shape of stars—spun towards the drone bed, ripping and slicing through their shelter wall of boxes. The sharp blades pierced clean through, and only by lying flat did she and Toshi keep from becoming pincushions.

When the star-swarm passed, Lotus shoved her hands back into the box and told Toshi, "Shoot while I distract him!" Grabbing an armful of the box's contents, she shouted at Trollic. "Here, have some raw calamari!"

With all her vempar strength, she threw squid after squid at the flying bounty hunter, the sea creatures sailing through the air like spears.

The squid pelted the beast, making him swerve left and right, and Toshi used the distraction to fire off well-aimed shots.

Trollic's jetpack suddenly flared along the side, leaking fuel from holes. He descended, cursing, and glared murder at them while he was forced to land far, far below.

Toshi sat back, breathing hard, and Lotus let her feet dangle over the edge as the drone continued its mechanical flight as if nothing had happened.

"Sad to see such good food go to waste," she muttered.

A strange noise came from Toshi, which she realized was a chuckle.

"I knew you had a sense of humor hidden in there, somewhere, Lollipop."

7

MOUNTAINS ROSE AND FELL TO THEIR left before the drone began to finally descend. A highway stretched below, and there appeared a chain of inns, restaurants, and whatnot for a traveler's stop.

It was to one of those restaurants that the drone lowered and landed on a concrete bay; Udon's Noodle Restaurant read the painted letters. Lotus and Toshi hid behind the boxes as a man came out to meet the drone.

The man texted something on his miPhone and lifted his cap to scratch his forehead before his gaze then lifted to the drone's bed and the devastation of bullet holes, spilled contents, and altogether missing boxes. He stood frozen, mouth opening and closing.

"If I had the money, I'd pay you back. Sorry!" Lotus shouted. She and Toshi ran from the drone and toward the wooded hills behind the restaurant.

They had almost reached the trees when a blur flashed by and the man with the cap appeared in their path.

Lotus halted, flapping her arms not to lose balance. The man crossed his burly arms and tilted his head, the brim of the cap no longer hiding his face. "Think you can wreck my shipment and get away with it?" he said, scanning them up and down. Toshi's hand neared his holster. "Don't get trigger-happy, boy. Hands up where I can see them! Something smells fishy, and it isn't the good sea food you ruined."

"I didn't want to waste it, either," said Lotus mournfully. "All that perfectly good squid used up to save our lives." Toshi rolled his eyes and stilled his hand, though he didn't raise it.

The man's gaze narrowed. "You've got a wig on," he noted. "Hey, are you that pair who's been causing trouble on trains? I saw the surveillance footage on TV. What were you doing, fighting a nasty trollic? They say it was some dressed-up creep, but I know a trollic when I see one."

Lotus sensed Toshi was ready to run again; she agreed with that strategy. And at a nod, they sprinted off to the left, leaving the man behind—or so they thought, before he appeared standing in front of them again.

She stared at the guy openly, his speed too unnatural. Almost like a…a…

"That's right." The man grinned under their tense and troubled stares. "I'm a vempar, like you, girl. In disguise." Pointed ears showed from under the cap.

Lotus gawked. Her mouth bobbed open and closed like a fish.

Another vempar—there was another person here like her!

Minutes of talking later found them all carrying boxes off the delivery drone and tucking them into the back garage. The drone, once empty, automatically took flight and left for its home base.

"Even if Trollic Tracker can't see these boxes, he's still going to check this whole area," Lotus voiced her thoughts.

"Well, he's got a bunch of inns and other restaurants to go snooping through down this highway, first. Name's Shino, by the way."

"Lotus, Toshi," she gestured.

They followed Shino indoors to the kitchens, where chefs were working to fill orders. The cacophony of sweet and savory smells made her stomach give in to furious growls.

"Oi, Tsuki, two ramen bowls here!" called Shino.

Someone answered "*Hai!*" as he placed she and Toshi at a back table where staff took lunch, currently empty. "He talk much?" Shino indicated Toshi with a thumb.

"Uh, only when few people are around. It's complicated."

"Huh."

Tsuki brought two large white bowls and plopped them down. Lotus's vision nearly glazed over in delight at the noodles, soft boiled egg, bone broth, slices of beef and cooked greens, all working together to make one amazing bowl of ramen. She ate hungrily, savoring each bite.

"Running from the mafia's a pretty darn daring thing to do, kid. Where do you plan on going from here?" Shino made conversation while they ate.

"Do you know the legend of the Beorgan Society?" Lotus spoke around noodles.

"Ah, the story of a world for Altered kind." Shino glanced at the ceiling fondly, rubbing his round chin. "I never much believed it, though."

"It's real. I have proof, and that's where we're going," Lotus affirmed, and ignored Toshi's rebuking glare and hand on her wrist, wanting her to keep quiet. "Would you want to come with us?" she asked.

Shino's gaze took in the kitchen and the workers for several moments. "Nah, I couldn't leave. Even if such a place were real. This world is my home, good or bad, and I want to be a refuge for the Altered who live in it."

Lotus chewed on an egg slice and nodded, a part of her wondering what it would be like to own a ramen restaurant and make a safe haven for Altered. She imagined that scenario, and at every turn the mafia or Trollic were not far behind.

"I'm not saying you shouldn't go look to see if the legend is true, and get out while you still can," said Shino. "That just isn't meant for me. We all have different paths we must walk, or so my granny used to say."

When they finished their meal, Shino ushered them into his small office room. "Rest up here and keep out of sight. Won't do you any good traveling about in daylight. Wait until after sunset. Looks like you could use a nap, anyway."

"But Trollic—"

"Has his face all over the news, same as you. Though people think it's a mask he's wearing." Shino left, closing the door. Lotus decided to do as suggested and take a nap, though looking over at Toshi, he was busy observing through a window in the door.

"Toshi, what are you doing?" she said, irritated.

"JUST BECAUSE HE'S ALTERED DOESN'T MEAN HE'S TRUSTWORTHY."

"You have to doubt everything and everybody, don't you?"

"*YES. THAT'S HOW I SURVIVED.*"

She closed her mouth against what she'd been going to say, and for some reason felt embarrassed. "You haven't said much about yourself. You already know *my* story, which isn't fair."

Toshi didn't answer, his face to the window.

Tired, she laid her head down on the carpeted floor. The whine of a police siren, small at first, drew near. She tensed, and Toshi grabbed the knob of the door. But the siren continued past.

The day faded to evening, and into sunset, and the bustle of dinner time beyond the walls of the room grew loud. Shino brought them another meal of ramen, and told them the police had been wandering about, asking questions and showing surveillance photos of the three train raid suspects.

"Train raid?" repeated Lotus, incredulous.

"Well, they've got to call it something, I suppose." Shino dumped a handful of syringes with needle tips into her lap, their contents glowing blue. "Here's a supply of life-energy, so you won't be needing to worry about it while you travel."

"Life-energy in a tube, that's convenient. Thanks!" She stuffed them in her pockets. "...Not sure if I should ask how you got them?"

"Secret hospital donations in the area." He waved her worry away and went to the door. "I'll let you know when it's safe to leave."

Once the dinner crowd had mostly gone for the night, and those who lingered were more interested in their *sake* drinks than anything else, Shino led Toshi and Lotus out the back.

Stars were being swallowed up by clouds rolling in.

Lotus drew the jacket hood over her wig, and Toshi raised

the collar of his borrowed coat.

"Keep along the highway south. It's a long walk, but you'll reach Karatsu City, and wherever you're going from there," said Shino.

Lotus gave him a quick hug. "Thanks for the help! And…keep safe." Though, she knew keeping safe wasn't much possible for their kind. And with the threat of war and other disasters looming on the news, she wished she could take all of the Altered in Japan away with her.

"We'll be fine, Lotus-chan. Even if the world goes mad for a bit, we Altered know how to wait things out." Shino winked.

She followed Toshi toward the highway road and waved back at Shino.

The night closed in around them as they left the parking lot lights and hiked through the brush running along the highway.

They kept a distance from the passing cars and road lights, keeping the road just in view to follow it while keeping themselves out of sight. The land was hilly except for patches of farmland they crossed and the occasional rest-stop buildings.

A drop of rain flicked Lotus on the nose, and she rubbed it. A white line streaked across the sky and thunder growled soon after. More raindrops pattered the ground, and she prepared herself for a wet journey. Toshi's coat didn't have a hood.

She listened to the patter of rain while they walked, and then to something that whistled through the air, a sudden yet quiet noise.

By the time she recognized it as a threat, the rope and grapple had caught Toshi's legs, wrapping around them.

He fell, and she turned in horror to see Trollic Tracker's dark form against the backdrop of clouds and field.

She heard the brush of shurikens through the air and rolled Toshi out of the way. The blades slashed lines past her back.

Toshi sawed at the rope around his legs with a knife, "*GO!*" he urged her. She shook her head, helping tear the rope off.

More shurikens came. Toshi got to his feet and they ran together in a crouch.

There weren't many trees here. The only shelter looked to be a plot of oddly shaped stones and sculptures off the highway. They ran for it; she used her strength to move faster and pull Toshi along.

They soon stumbled onto a gravel path and entered a maze of strange stones. Under a flash of lightning, she realized they were in a cemetery.

She didn't have time to be creeped out but hurried behind stone crosses and tall rectangles, everything shadows and grays in the mix of night and lightning. The rain became an even downpour.

A shuriken chipped the headstone behind her. Toshi motioned for her to keep going while he pulled out one gun and used a double headstone for cover. She heard his gun fire off two rounds.

It was greeted by a blast from Trollic's bigger gun. The double headstone exploded.

Toshi's gun fired from a different position, and Trollic's gun answered again.

Lotus continued on in a crawl, all the while hearing Dad's voice and seeing Mom's smile, the cemetery summoning up memories.

Lightning flashed and there appeared a foot by her right hand. She flung herself back with a scream.

The foot was attached to a tall statue—not Trollic. But her scream had given away her position.

The statue exploded in a gun blast, and chunks rained down on her. Lotus crawled from the spot and got to her feet before sprinting into a run.

The rain made it hard to see, and she hoped also made it impossible for a gun to hit true. Where was Toshi? She didn't want them to get separated like this! She ducked through rows of brightly painted mausoleums and dark stone lanterns, and the rain grew louder, falling in sheets and blown by the wind.

She wrenched open the lock of a mausoleum and took cover inside, shaking off water, then peeked out, hoping to glimpse the hauk.

She waited, silent. Lightning cast a shadow upon the grass nearby. She held her breath and watched as the shadow lengthened and moved nearer. She readied her trembling fists as the shadow came to the door.

"Lo…" came an indiscernible sound, like from a throat not used to speaking. She opened the door.

Relief flooded through her as Toshi ducked inside, pressing his back to the fancy wood door. The small space was made smaller by the coffin displayed on pedestals at the room's center. A flash of lightning let her see colors painted on the walls, symbols of lotus flowers and birds.

There they waited, not speaking, not daring to move or risk making a sound. It felt like hours ticked by; the rain increased and decreased at intervals. She doubted she'd be able to hear if Trollic approached, but she focused on listening and smelling the air anyway, some old incense and decay interfering.

Toshi peered through the narrow gap between the door and the frame. After a minute, his neck went rigid.

"HE'S COMING." The computer voice was turned down to the lowest setting.

Lotus moved to peer out another gap. Trollic's shadow moved among the mausoleums, checking inside them one by one.

Her heart sank; they were trapped, and not just in this tomb. They would be followed out of the cemetery wherever they tried to run.

"I don't think I'm strong enough to beat him…" she heard herself admit, her hands trembling again.

Toshi spared her a glance. *"THERE IS ONE POSSIBLE WAY OUT."*

Toshi dropped his hand, giving her the signal as Trollic forced open the door of the next mausoleum over. Lotus kicked a hole through the back of the tomb's decorated wood wall at the same time—using Trollic's noise to mask the sound—and she silently apologized to the resident.

She crawled through the gap, Toshi after her, and she stayed close to his side ducking behind stone lanterns in the pounding rain. Urgency drove her like a whip, not knowing if Trollic Tracker had heard the breaking wood or not.

A bullet soon blasted the headstone five feet from them, giving her the answer.

Toshi pulled back and veered course; she followed in a crouch.

The grass ended at a gravel path, and Toshi paused behind a square headstone and incense tray. He spotted and pointed to their goal: a storm drain grate in the path.

She hurried to the grate, lifting and setting it aside, then realized Toshi wasn't behind her anymore.

She looked about frantically, sitting on her heels.

Gunfire came off to the right—he was leading Trollic away from her.

She froze, torn as to what to do: go help, or get in the storm drain as he'd wanted.

Her body made the decision for her, dropping into the drain tunnel while her mind battled over what to do. She pressed her back to the damp, mildew tunnel wall, rain pouring in from above and from other drain grates, creating a river that flowed past her thighs.

She waited…flinched at each gunshot…

And then, there was nothing making a sound but the wind and rain above.

Lotus stilled, worry flaring in her gut. As each second ticked by she struggled to decide whether to tug the grate back over the storm drain hole and flee with the water or continue waiting, to see if Toshi might make it back.

The crunch of gravel arrived too fast for her to decide, and a dark form dropped into the tunnel with her. Lightning glinted off the device in Toshi's ears.

She quickly reached up, grabbed the grate with her strengthened fingers and dragged it back over the opening, plunging the tunnel into further darkness.

Together, they waded through the tunnel river that was steadily rising to their chests, pressing their hands to the right tunnel wall for balance and assurance as everything became blackness and water. She clung her free left hand to Toshi's coat, even if it made her feel silly.

A bit of lightning slanted in through a passing drain grate, casting strange shadows. The darkness grew again, and they hurried past.

Lotus didn't know how long they waded and trudged through the tunnel, except that she was chilled to the bone and clothes clung like paste to her skin.

The water level rose to her shoulders, now. She kept her grip on Toshi's coat and could feel his strength waning despite how he pressed on.

"We can't anymore," she spoke for the first time in the darkness, even then a whisper. "This tunnel's going to fill up soon."

Toshi slowed; a faint gray light had revealed a drain grate ahead.

Lotus pushed on the grate with her palms, silently praying that they'd made it far enough away from the cemetery, and the grate slid back.

With a grip and a jump, she hoisted herself out of the tunnel. While Toshi came up, she took in their surroundings and observed a little village around them. There was no way to be sure how far from the cemetery it was, but she spotted the highway not far off.

They needed a dry place and rest. She spotted a little thatch roof barn and grabbed Toshi's arm to pull him along toward it without a word.

Avoiding what noisy puddles they could, she unlatched the door, and they found a spot among hay piles to sit and dry off. Toshi coughed and shivered for a while.

She was cold but knew her vempar body wasn't as affected by it as his. She wished she had a dry coat or something to give him, instead piling dry hay around him. She busied wringing the water out of her hair and jacket and his coat, also yanking off their wigs and plopping them on the straw to hopefully dry. She rested her arms on her knees and listened to the rain.

"You know, I once saw a young hauk boy, years ago. He was in a circus, and he did all sorts of tricks in the air... I could tell he loved being up there, flying." She half regretted saying it, but the thought had been on her mind.

Toshi stared at the barn wall, and his eyes looked moist. He turned his head to the side away from her, but spoke, *"I WAS IN A CIRCUS."*

Lotus didn't feel too surprised. "That was you I saw?"

"MOST LIKELY."

"How did…" she started to ask, then realized how sensitive the question might be and stopped.

Toshi didn't move, still turned away and shivering. *"THERE WAS A GROUP OF US HAUKS, ONCE,"* he said, and her attention went all to him. *"WE TRAVELED TOGETHER, LIVED TOGETHER, UNTIL THE NIGHT WHEN WE WERE ATTACKED."* He paused. *"HUMANS KILLED THEM AND CUT OFF THEIR WINGS—THAT WAS ALL THEY WANTED, THE WINGS TO FETCH A HIGH PRICE. I WAS A CHILD, HIDING UNDER A BASKET MY MOTHER HAD THROWN OVER ME. WHEN THE HUMANS LEFT, I CAME OUT, AND…NO ONE ELSE WAS ALIVE."*

He shifted to observe the ceiling. *"I WANDERED FOR DAYS, UNTIL ANOTHER ALTERED FOUND ME AND BROUGHT ME TO THAT TRAVELING CIRCUS. I WOULDN'T HAVE HAD FOOD OR SHELTER OTHERWISE…"*

"Did they…treat you well?"

"WELL ENOUGH TO LIVE, AS LONG AS I PROVED USEFUL AND BROUGHT IN MONEY WITH MY FLYING ACTS. BUT THAT LIFE ENDED WHEN I WAS ATTACKED BY A HUMAN WHO HACKED MY WING OFF."

Emotion couldn't fill his computer voice, but she could feel it all the same.

"HE WOULD HAVE TAKEN BOTH, BUT A CIRCUS MEMBER SCARED THE MAN OFF…I NO LONGER COULD BRING IN MONEY WITH MY ACTS. I TRIED TO LEARN

OTHER TALENTS BUT FAILED. AND THAT'S WHEN I WAS SOLD TO KURO."

Lotus fought back tears. He'd stopped talking, and she reached her hand to his, patting it before lacing her fingers through his. He acknowledged the gesture with a light brush from his thumb.

"THE SKY WAS MY HOME. I CAN NEVER SOAR IT WITH MY OWN WINGS AGAIN."

She let her head rest lightly against his shoulder. She could feel the great sense of loss, like a piece of his soul torn away. "I'm sorry, Toshi… You know, someday you might find a new technology that can help. Scientists have been experimenting with growing limbs and organs—and a wing wouldn't be too far out."

"EXCEPT THAT WE'RE TRYING TO LEAVE THIS WORLD."

She chewed her lip. "Yeah. I don't think before I talk, do I?"

He shrugged. *"THE THREAT OF WAR WILL HALT ANY MEDICAL PROGRESS, ANYWAYS… I AM DRY ENOUGH. WE SHOULD MOVE ON."*

A crack in the wood plank wall showed them the rain had slowed.

Yes, they had to keep ahead of Trollic Tracker—*if* they were still ahead; there was no safe way to find out.

8

THEY KEPT AT A BRISK PACE, FOLLOWING the highway while keeping a greater distance from it. Gray streaked the sky when the sun finally crested the rolling landscape. The wigs were dry enough to wear—a good thing, as Karatsu's cityscape in the distance grew.

The highway followed the coast, and Lotus marveled at the blueness of the water and the salty smell on the breeze; who knew a breeze could be salty?

The clouds broke up, letting morning light through.

Toshi walked closer to the beach as it curved away from the highway. She trotted up to him. "Aren't we supposed to follow the highway?"

"THE COAST LEADS INTO THE CITY AND TO

KARATSU PORT. THIS IS FASTER, AND I'M HOPING WILL KEEP TROLLIC TRACKER OFF OUR TRAIL FOR A WHILE."

She nodded, trusting that he knew the lay of the land well enough. Taking off her shoes and socks, she dashed onto the sandy beach skipping and kicking sand, feeling how it squished beneath her toes.

Toshi watched her, and she shrugged up her arms. "You can't *feel* what sand feels like through a TV screen, okay? It's grittier than I thought."

She had a not-as-fun time getting the sand out from between her toes to put her socks and shoes back on.

A forest of trees soon rose around them following the coastline path: towers of pine trunks twisting up to the sky. *"A PINE GROVE. ONCE PUT HERE TO ACT AS A SEA WALL,"* Toshi said, as she tipped her head far back while they walked, observing the sparse canopy that the clusters of pine needles made, sunlight dappling through. The air smelled uniquely of sap and salt, both.

After a while, they came across a clearing and a large van that looked more like a mini set-up restaurant, complete with picnic tables and hungry tourists.

Toshi quickened his pace to move past, but Lotus's footsteps drew her towards the scent of food.

Toshi looked back and made an irritated sound.

"Money?" Lotus smiled sweetly at him.

"I SEE THE WAY TO YOUR HEART IS FOOD." Toshi handed her yen bills with a frown.

"Can't travel on an empty stomach! Besides, we blend in with tourists." Lotus skipped over to wait in line. The sign read Karatsu Burger, and the meat smell enticed her to order two of the burgers.

Once she had them in hand, she moved past the tables back to Toshi and continued their walk while eating, tossing the second burger to him.

He smirked, catching it.

He had a cute smirk, the kind that dimpled one cheek. His eyes had a new spark to them today, too. Perhaps surviving the night in the rain with a killer on their tail had done the trick. Or maybe…

She caught him looking at her. "What?"

He shrugged, glancing away. *"YOU HAVE A FUNNY WAY OF EATING."*

"Eh? You wanna poke fun at my eating habits?" She frowned around a bite.

"YOUR FACE LIGHTS UP WHEN YOU HAVE FOOD."

She was about to say something smart back when he added: *"IT'S CUTE."*

Her cheeks went red. It must have made him feel awkward because his pace quickened, and he didn't make eye-contact. After the burger, she used one of the life-energy syringes from Shino and felt more rejuvenated.

The tranquil pine grove came to an end, sadly, and the path broke out between buildings and homes, at the end of which was a bridge.

Lotus listened to the rush and breath of the waves as they crossed over an inlet of sea water.

An old Japanese castle rose ahead to their right, now a historic site and museum. She admired the tiered levels, stacked almost like a pyramid, and the upward curved tips of the roofs.

They kept to the edge of Karatsu City, following the beach and taking cover in the lines of trees that sprang up. It was a long walk, especially when the heat of noon came. Even the ocean breeze didn't help much.

When the beach ended, they were forced to follow streets and signs. Lotus's feet were Healing blisters by the time Toshi pointed, "*KARATSU PORT,*" the light in his tired eyes renewed.

A spark of thrill ran through Lotus. Here, they would finally catch their ride to Iki Island. The location of the portal was getting closer.

A ferryboat's horn cried, and Toshi hurried her to the booth to buy tickets. "Um, two for the ferry to Iki Island, please?" She handed over the yen Toshi pushed at her.

A policeman walked back and forth through the port lobby.

They kept inconspicuous; she made sure her orange hair didn't peek out from under the dark wig as they trotted out to the ferryboat as it was preparing to leave, and they dashed aboard.

She chose a seat near the prow and felt the ferry's engine when it rumbled and began moving them briskly out of the docks.

There was a sense of relief being out on the water, headed to Iki. It was too late for Trollic Tracker to catch up to them, now. He didn't have his jetpack anymore, and he couldn't be sure where it was they were headed.

The breeze cooled the farther the boat sailed across the salty waters, then began warming again when land came into view up ahead. Iki was all green rolling hills, sand beaches, and patches of rising towns.

The ferry pulled into port at a city, which looked to be only a cluster of large, modern buildings and then country shops and houses—as if the people wanted their island to advance only to a certain degree. Tall palm trees swayed gently overhead while they stepped off onto the dock and headed into the streets.

Toshi made his way to a bus stop sign, but Lotus spotted a pick-up truck whose owner had just finished emptying out the back. She skipped over to the weighty man, making sure her ears were kept beneath her wig.

"Excuse me, sir?" She caught his attention. "Are you heading north today? Me and my brother could use a lift, and we'd pay you well for it." She made sure to smile without showing the points of her canine fangs.

The man regarded her, squinting his already slanted, wrinkled eyes. "*Hai*, I'm headed north back home. You can ride in the back of the truck until we reach Ashibeura City."

"*Arigatou gozaimasu!*" Lotus bowed in thanks. People in the countryside seemed a lot nicer than city folk, just like in the TV shows.

She trotted to where Toshi stood waiting and told him about her achievement. "It'll be roomier than a stuffy bus, and fewer chances that somebody will see through our disguise."

Toshi didn't look pleased, but then he never really looked pleased about anything, so she grabbed his wrist and pulled him along to the truck.

The hairs on the nape of her neck suddenly stood on end, and she looked up at the buildings. Just for a second, it felt like she was being watched. She spotted some locals observing the tourists who got off the ferry, and she again made sure her ears were hidden.

She hurried her footsteps to the truck and handed the driver the yen Toshi was going to use for a bus. The truck bed was wide and roomy, and a little bumpy as the engine sprang to life beneath their seats. The truck rumbled over the crudely paved path leading out of the city and into the island's interior.

Palm trees became fewer, and fields of barley took their place. Each breeze rippled like a wave through the stalks. The blue sky stretched from horizon to horizon, the hills making it uneven, and Lotus caught the scent of farmland.

The land opened wide to odd structures, and she sat upright to get a better look as they drove past: they looked like huts and old houses and barns, but all of them smothered under heavy thatch roofs. Some you could barely see the walls, the ceiling thatch slanted so low to the ground. The letters on a sign she could pick out said something about a historic site and museum. She rested her chin on her arms on the edge of the truck bed and watched the thatch roofs roll by.

After more trees and fields and pretty patches of yellow flowers, the peaks of Ashibeura buildings disrupted the landscape. The city looked even smaller than the first as the truck pulled up to a curb.

She and Toshi hopped off, and she waved as the driver continued his journey. The city lay along the coast, and sunlight played over the little waves that came rolling in.

"I'm starving. I can't remember the last time I tasted food," said Lotus.

She caught Toshi's eye roll.

"I DON'T HAVE MUCH MONEY LEFT."

Lotus let her lips pout and eyebrows droop.

"NO."

She made a tear well in the corner of her eye. "Not even for one steamed bun?"

He regarded her, arms crossed, then made a sound like a sigh. *"FINE. WAIT HERE."*

She plopped down on a bench and crossed her knees, flashing a grin. Toshi slipped inside a fast-food building. She kicked her feet back and forth, then tapped her toes together, the salty air somehow making her hungrier.

The sun was setting, and shadows played along the harbor.

She didn't notice one of the shadows move—until it was

too late, and a clawed hand clamped over her mouth from behind.

Lotus tried to open her eyes. For some odd reason, it felt like a huge effort, as if her whole body had been sapped of all its strength.

Once she managed to see, the sun was setting off to her left in a display of golden and dark clouds, and the wind flapped her orange curls against her cheek. City rooftops spread left and right, and she couldn't understand how, until she realized she was no longer on the ground but high on a flat rooftop.

She peered over the edge: down at the harbor and the streets running along it.

A darkly clad figure with creamy brown skin came out into the street, stared at a bench for one moment, then looked sharply both ways down the street.

She wanted to call out to Toshi. Why was she so weak? She tried to move her arms, but they held firmly behind her.

"Don't make me drug you again," spoke a gruff, deep voice at her back. Her arms were gripped in place by someone, and she didn't need to turn her head to know who.

Lotus forced her throat to make a sound. "Tosh…!" she called, though it sounded so weak and strained. Still, Toshi's head snapped up and she knew he'd spotted them on the roof.

The bag in his hand fell to the ground and he ran towards the building; she briefly lamented the discarded food.

Worry pounded in her ears; what could Trollic Tracker be up to? Why lure them on a roof? Why didn't he just finish her off?

And for that matter, how the heck did he get here right when they did?

The stairwell door flung open and Toshi slipped onto the roof, halting opposite her and Trollic. His gloves were off, and she could see the thick, black nails of his hauk race as each hand grasped the grip of his guns. She noted his brief glance at the roof's edge—the height a reminder of his lost wing.

"WHY WERE YOU WAITING ON A ROOF FOR ME?" Toshi demanded.

Lotus gaped at him. Weren't there more important things to discuss, like freeing her?

Trollic let out a chuckle that sounded like the grunts of a bull through his tusked jaws. "I didn't want to, little hauk, trust me. I'd rather have slit your throat from the shadows. But Kuro sent me a message with an offer to give you."

Toshi cocked his head to listen, and Lotus's breath hitched.

"Kuro is willing to forgive and take you back, *if* you return peacefully with the vempar girl," said Trollic.

Toshi regarded him, clearly doubtful.

One of Trollic's hands let go of her arm to reach inside a pocket and toss out a card. The card landed by Toshi's boot. He kept his eye on them and bent to pick it up: an official pardon, signed by Kuro himself.

"THINGS CAN GO BACK TO THE WAY THEY WERE?"

"That's right. Kuro needs the money this vempar brat brings in, so he's decided to be generous."

Toshi stared at the card, unmoving, brow pinched in thought.

A new sense of panic fingered Lotus as she battled her body's weakened state. She thought to Toshi's earlier doubts, his words about how unlikely it was that the portal existed, that it could just be another fairy tale.

Would Toshi accept a realistic offer rather than some blind hope of a mythical portal?

Toshi slipped the card into his pocket and shrugged off the coat and wig disguise. *"I DON'T WANT TO BE ON THE RUN FOR THE REST OF MY LIFE. I WOULD RATHER RETURN."*

Lotus felt her heart drop; her knees gave out and she sat hard on the roof floor.

All of this had been for nothing. She was so near to the X on the map yet would never be able to see her hope realized. Toshi was betraying her, and after all they had survived through.

"HOW DID YOU KNOW WE WOULD COME HERE?" Toshi asked as he drew near, pulling on his gloves.

Trollic tossed a crumpled paper. "The map I took from you had a crease mark on Iki Island, as if someone kept touching that spot. You were already headed south-west, so it wasn't that hard to figure out." He dragged Lotus up to her feet. "Sure you want to give in and work as Kuro's slave again, little hauk? I would relish having a reason to kill you here."

"I'M SURE YOU WOULD." Toshi nodded his chin over to Lotus. *"WHAT'S WRONG WITH HER?"*

"Tranquilizer dose—enough to kill an elephant. It should keep her obedient for a while."

Lotus vaguely fingered a needle mark on her neck. She fought not to let her eyelids droop, the sting of betrayal and anger writhing inside her.

Toshi wouldn't meet her gaze. He headed into the roof stairwell, and Trollic dragged her along with him to the open stair door.

Trollic had reached the first step when Toshi's sudden kick met his chest. And in the second that Trollic unbalanced, Toshi crouched and swiped his leg in a move that knocked Trollic back off his feet.

Lotus blinked, her head trying to register what had just happened, and Toshi grabbed her hand.

"HURRY!"

She stumbled forward, but a hand caught her ankle and threw her backwards, sending her sprawling across the roof and yanking her from Toshi's grasp.

She lifted herself up on an elbow and saw Trollic's gauntleted fist strike the side of Toshi's head. There was a loud *crack*.

Toshi stumbled towards her several steps before collapsing to his knees. His hands gripped the sides of his head, and an excruciating groan exited his throat, the agony making her shiver.

In horror, she realized that the device attached in his ears, which allowed him to hear and spoke for him, had been damaged and was crackling.

Trollic leered around his yellowed tusks like a demon. "I will relish this."

He approached, unsheathing the katana sword at his back, salty wind whipping his wild black hair.

Lotus balled her hands into fists and forced her body to stand. Images of her dad, the spear thrust through his chest, flashed through her mind. She would *not* let that happen again!

She focused on Toshi, in agony on the floor, gathered her courage with a silent prayer, and placed herself between him and the approaching beast.

"You want to die, too, like your daddy?" Trollic sneered.

She held her ground, feet apart in the ready stance she'd seen martial artists do online. She didn't have practice fighting, but she did have vempar strength.

Trollic angled the katana. "You'll live if I cut off a few limbs, won't you? I'm sure Kuro won't mind."

He sprinted forward, blade raised.

Lotus hopped to the right, and his momentum carried him past her. He turned sharply on his heels and swung the blade.

Lotus dodged left. The tip cut a line across her forearm which she barely felt.

The action reminded her of the life-energy syringes Shino had given her, and she snatched the one she'd stored inside her boot and injected the needle into her thigh. The wooziness of the tranquilizer began to fade, and she dodged another slice and two thrusts of the katana.

"Try dodging this!" Trollic Tracker snarled and with his other hand pulled out a gun. Bullets hit her legs as she ran in a circle around him, and the katana swiped at her so she couldn't get close.

She used another syringe. If she could just get rid of one of those weapons…

She made a dash straight for him, ignoring the burning sting of bullets, arm shielding her heart.

Trollic raised the katana for a downward slice.

At the last second, as the blade's edge came down on her, she stepped slightly to the right, tucked her left elbow in, and gripping her wrist for added strength with her other hand, thrust her elbow out and into the flat of the blade as it swung down—breaking the katana in two, the force ripping the hilt out of Trollic's grasp and sending the pieces whistling away through the air.

Trollic looked stunned for a moment, then aimed his gun while his other hand reached for a new weapon under his cloak. But in that moment, Lotus balled vempar strength up in her right fist and delivered a punch to Trollic's gut that broke through the armor plate he wore and sent him reeling back.

While he was still staggering backwards, a figure rushed past Lotus, and the twin blades of Toshi's gun-swords buried themselves into the bounty hunter's now exposed flesh.

Trollic screamed and growled. Toshi yanked the blades free before he could grab them and sent Trollic rolling to the edge of the roof with a kick.

Trollic staggered, trying to stand. Toshi roared, flapping his single wing and axe-kicked Trollic—sending him falling over the edge.

Lotus held her aching arm as she neared the edge, looking down at the spot of ocean water and hearing the large *splash*. She sat back on her heels, panting.

Toshi slumped to the ground, his chest rising and falling.

"Are you okay?" she managed to ask. When he remained quiet, staring up at the gathering dark of the sky, she knew he could no longer hear or speak.

She crawled and sat down beside him, watching as the sun lowered, and at some point sleep overtook her.

9

Lotus woke to the smell of onions and the rhythmic thump of chopping. A wood-beam ceiling stared down at her as she cracked her eyelids open.

She sat up, every joint in her creaking in protest. At the center of the single room she lay in burned a fire pit, a cauldron bubbling over it while someone stirred in freshly cut onions.

She barely registered the person, her attention going to the body lying nearby, instead.

"Toshi!" She moved to press her palm to his forehead. He felt clammy. The device that had wrapped behind his head from ear to ear was missing; only the small, flat pieces implanted in his ears where the device had connected remained, and a damp cloth was pressed over a badly bruised bump.

Tears stung her eyes, and she fought a losing battle not to let emotions take over.

"*Daijoubu*. He'll recover. Though it may help if you do a little Healing on that whack to the head he's got."

Lotus turned on her knees, now fully taking in the person sitting by the fire:

Long red hair tied back, and wearing a simple kimono, but nothing beyond that was normal about the woman. Instead of human ears, she had the fluffy, triangular ears of a red fox, and a matching bushy tail swished across the bamboo-carpet floor.

"What...are you?"

"How rude. Do not all vempars learn manners, these days?" tsked the female Altered in a high, almost child-like voice. "I'm a kitsune. And my name, which is what you should've asked for first, is Ikue."

Lotus sat on her knees and bowed. "Thank you for taking care of us, Ikue-san. But how...I mean, the last thing I remember is that I was on a roof, and..."

"Yes, I saw that trollic beast fall—quite a splash that made! I had to run up and see who'd done him in; I'm curious like that. Of course, all I found were two unconscious teenagers." She tapped the spoon on the cauldron's lip and set it down, reaching for bowls. "Unfortunately, my heart was too soft to let humans find you lying prone like that and do who-knows-what to you."

"Thank you." Lotus meant it, with every fiber of her being.

"Well." Ikue sniffed and handed her a bowl of soup. "This is my little home in the mountain forest. Hope that doesn't put your travel plans to ruin. What're you doing here on Iki, anyway?"

Lotus took the bowl of beef broth soup gratefully; she set it aside and placed her hands on Toshi's head, Healing the damage there.

"We came to find the portal of the Beorgan Society," she said quietly, guilt stirring in her as Toshi's head wound Healed.

"Oh, that. It's been decades since someone came looking for the legend."

Lotus perked up, the Healing finished. "You know where it is?"

"Ha. No." Ikue flapped her hand. "But I once saw a little group who passed through searching for it." She tipped her bowl, sipping without a spoon. Lotus returned to the bowl she'd been given and slurped it down in gulps.

Toshi stirred and grunted. Lotus moved back to his side.

He blinked awake, charcoal bangs damp along his temples. He saw her and slowly sat up.

"How does it feel?" Lotus asked. He gingerly touched his head, then his ears. She again forgot he couldn't hear her.

Panic flashed across his face before he concealed it under a blank mask. He looked to her, tapped his ear with a finger, and touched her hand.

Lotus shook her head. "I cannot make you hear again," she mouthed as slowly and clearly as possible for him to read her lips. "Healing does not work like that. It cannot fix something you were born with."

His gaze turned to the bamboo floor, and she handed him a bowl of soup, which he took and ate almost mechanically. He glanced around the place: at the window and each dark corner, and at Ikue; he looked as if he feared something might sneak up on him without him knowing.

He focused on Ikue, glancing at Lotus, and she tried to explain how Ikue had helped them.

"Is his hearing device fixable?" she asked the kitsune lady, who watched them with curiosity.

"No. That's why I took it off. Crazy thing was sparking and liable to start a fire." She indicated the metal pile by the wall. Lotus frowned; it really was beyond repair. And something like that was too expensive to simply go and buy. Kuro must have had it made specially for him when he started working for the mafia.

Toshi didn't bother to look at it but remained tense.

"Do you know if that group you saw ever found the portal or not?" she asked Ikue, who shrugged.

"No idea. But I didn't see them return. Of course, they could've taken a different route back and I wouldn't have known." Ikue gathered the empty bowls. "There's a hot spring out back. Why don't you both clean up, so you can resemble civilized beings?"

Lotus's mouth puckered, but a hot bath did sound refreshing.

Towel wrapped around her, Lotus slid the back door open, and there a pool of milky-green water steamed the air.

She found a bucket and rinsed herself off first, as was custom, before stepping into the pool. She sunk down into the milky warmth and breathed in the misting steam.

Ah, this was luxurious.

She could've stayed in there for hours, but knew she'd become a boiled lobster if she did.

Climbing back out reluctantly, a thought that the portal might not be there, might not be real, nagged at the back of her mind. That Toshi's sacrifices could be for nothing. That in the end, Kuro would have them both under his thumb again.

She shook the water from her hair, making raindrops.

Once Lotus and Toshi were clean and dressed in local *haori* jackets and *hakama* pants, which Ikue insisted upon, they were ready to depart. Thankfully, there were pockets for Lotus to stuff the remaining life-energy syringes in.

Ikue finished tying on a brown kimono. The fox lady motioned with her hand, and they followed her outside into the rocky woods which kept her small home concealed. "I'll guide you to Tatsunoshima Island, since I've nothing better to do this day," she said. "That's the name of the little island marked on your map near Iki."

"Won't you come with us to the portal?" Lotus asked.

"*Iie*, who would be here to scare the local children, and keep the kitsune legends alive? I so enjoy the new Halloween holiday foreigners have brought in." Ikue tipped her head back with a gleeful grin.

Lotus shivered. "What kind of person are you?"

"I thought we already established that."

Beside Lotus, Toshi scanned the woods, now and then looking over his shoulder and up to the canopy. Watching him made her realize how much she relied on her hearing: to inform her of her surroundings, to know if someone was creeping up behind her.

Toshi must feel as if he was partially blind to the world around him, now. His gaze met her stare, and she quickly looked away.

Twin shrine posts rose on their right, the red paint peeling and faded. Stone steps snaked from the posts and off into the woods; there parked beside them was a horse and cart.

Ikue patted the black horse's sleek back. "Hop on!" She stepped lithely onto the front cart seat and sat on a cushion, next pulling out a gourd container full of something. She took a drink while Lotus and Toshi situated themselves inside the cart.

"You just happen to have a horse and cart?" Lotus asked.

"Don't call Ryoma a horse!" snapped Ikue. "He's much more than that. Aren't you?"

The horse nodded, throwing what felt like a glare at Lotus.

"Um, sorry," Lotus mumbled.

"Take us to Tatsunoshima Island, my friend!" declared Ikue.

The horse—or whatever Ryoma was—neighed and reared up on his hindlegs. Black wings unfolded like scales from his neck and sides, and with a leap the horse dove forward down the path.

Lotus squealed and held on tight to the cart's side. Toshi's arm kept her from tumbling out when the horse suddenly went airborne and the cart dragged along after.

Ikue whooped, holding the gourd high.

The rush of air stung Lotus's eyes; trees shrunk, and the cart skimmed above the woods, rocking back and forth.

She bumped into Toshi's shoulder, and amusement lit his face. She stuck out her tongue, though glad to see a spark of humor return to him.

Whatever Ryoma was, his scaly wings carried them aloft over the wooded hills and fields, the sun making his black coat glisten. A flash of longing played across Toshi's face, the wind shoving back his hair.

It was a long flight over the trees and fields until the coast came into view and scent, shimmering green water and soft sand. Ryoma steered them left of a port city and skimmed across the sea.

"What if someone sees us?" Lotus shouted to Ikue, perched contentedly at the cart's front and flicking her fox tail.

"We'll look like a ghost cart at Ryoma's speed," said Ikue. "This is Iki, Japan: a place full of myths and folklore. Flying carts fit right in!"

Lotus had doubts about that.

They glided above the water, and she trailed her foot over the edge, leaving a long wake behind them.

A cruise boat appeared on their right, and Ryoma steered a sharp left, speeding off. Though, not before a little girl saw the flying cart and dropped a lollipop from her mouth.

Ikue waved her gourd and threw a kiss. The child watched, speechless.

"And so, the myths live on!" Ikue laughed.

The girl and boat faded from sight.

Lotus shared a look with Toshi, who shrugged.

Toshi himself looked like a myth beside her: dressed in kimono, his hawk wing folded behind him, and feathers mixed in his hair.

Tatsunoshima Island appeared before them not long after like a sparkling green jewel.

The cart skirted the beach, beginning a circle around the small island. "Does that crystal give any hint as to where on this island you wish to be?" Ikue asked.

Lotus shook her head, fingering the crystal. "All I know is the story says it's inside a cave."

"Heh, there're tons of caves here!"

Soon as Ikue said it, arches of stone rose out of the tropic foliage: eroded stacks and shapes of rock that seemed impossible for nature to craft.

The cart veered into a gorge snaking through the island. High walls of rock rose to either side, and the river splashed fiercely beneath them.

Lifting out, they crossed to an empty white beach and there the cart landed with a kick-up of sand.

Ryoma neighed and shook out his mane. Ikue hopped down and stashed away the gourd, and began picking up colorful shells, the kind Lotus had only ever seen in online stores. She fingered one that was wide and pink.

"Here's your starting point!" proclaimed the fox lady. "I'll give you three days to search the island before I come back to this beach. If you've found nothing and fall into depression, wait here and I'll return you to Iki. You can decide what you want to do with the rest of your lives from there."

"Such a boost of confidence you give us," said Lotus.

"I prefer the realistic approach."

The cart soon took flight, leaving Toshi and Lotus alone on the beach.

She stared after the cart for a while, and its crafty kitsune, before turning to face the island and eroded cliffs.

Toshi tapped her shoulder and pointed down the curving beach: a group of what looked like tourists was coming.

"Guess we start our search going to the *left*, then."

They followed the course of the beach, away from people, wading through water when beach disappeared to be replaced by rocks and cliffs.

At every cave and crevice they halted, ducked inside, and searched about. Toshi ran his hands along the gray and green rock, as if the walls might hide the secret.

Lotus had forgotten to ask Ikue for a pack of food. She was famished by the end of the day.

Toshi helped her scare a group of fish into the shallows and catch them. Skewered on sticks, the fish crisped over a little fire. It was chewy but decent enough.

When nightfall came and the dark wouldn't let them keep searching, they huddled inside a crevice and slept. Toshi tossed once in his sleep, something between a groan and a scream coming out, and he startled awake.

She didn't ask what nightmare it was, but wove her fingers through his, reassuring him with touch, a sense he still had.

By the next day's afternoon, they'd made a complete circle of the island.

Lotus could feel dread starting to trouble her breathing. They should have found it by now, right? Why would a necklace with a map be passed down for generations if it meant nothing?

Toshi patted her arm and indicated the island's center.

"You're right. There are more caves in the island's interior." She put on her smile, no matter how fake it felt.

They tried to cover the island one section at a time, and the day passed and the next one began, still with no discoveries or clues.

By the end of the third day, there was nowhere left to search, and Lotus sat down on a rock overlooking a cliff and the coast. Her breathing was a mess, and tears trickled down.

Crystal pendant in her fist, she thought of her parents, their sacrifice. Of Toshi's sacrifice.

She heard him climb up beside her, and the guilt brought her close to vomiting.

"I'm sorry, Toshi. This is all my fault," she mouthed. "You already lost your ability to fly, and now, because of me, you've lost even more… I ruined our lives for a hope that did not exist. You were right all along."

Toshi grabbed her hands and cupped them in his. He shook his head, eyes fixed on hers. His voice began to make sounds, trying to form the sounds into words, and his right hand pressed his throat to feel the vibrations of each word correctly. "Yu ere ight."

Lotus listened, translating the sounds: "You were right. You followed what God was telling you, and now we are free.

No more fighting. We live in peace on island."

Lotus shook her head. "Until Kuro discovers where we are."

"It's okay. I am happy to hide and run if it means no more a prisoner."

"But your hearing…"

"I manage. It's like before when I was with circus. I adapt."

Tears flooded her vision until she could no longer see.

She leaned forward and snatched Toshi in a hug, pulling him close, burying her wet face in his kimono. His hands rubbed her back and held the back of her head as she cried.

10

THE CRY OF A SEA BIRD WOKE HER. The sun was just beginning to crest the island's hills.

Toshi was still asleep on the rough ground, and she tried to be quiet when she stood and stretched—then remembered there was no need to be.

She climbed over rocks and walked for a bit, taking in the tropical view and rosy sky.

Her left foot slipped suddenly. She looked down to see why.

The ground there had dipped to a hole, no wider than her waist.

Getting on her knees, she tried to peer down inside it:

A hollowed-out space lay beneath, and dark shadows that hinted at tunnels.

Could this be…?

Lotus hopped to her feet and started back for Toshi.

A dark figure climbing over the cliff slope made her pause, the person heading towards them.

Twin horns glinted in the dawn and wild black hair rippled, his gait limping, and one of his arms wrapped up. Trollic Tracker.

"Toshi!" she shouted, before realizing again the uselessness.

Trollic would reach his sleeping form before she could.

Lotus grabbed a pebble and flung it hard at Toshi's leg.

The hauk sat up, wide-eyed and clutching his shin. When he spotted Trollic, he was on his feet, reaching for his gun and running to where she stood.

"You won't escape this time, sewer rats." Trollic's gray skin creased sneering lines around his yellowed tusks.

"How did you survive?" Lotus demanded.

Without listening for an answer, she grabbed Toshi's hand and pulled him backwards with her, step by step, until the hole in the ground was near their heels.

"I've survived worse than that." Trollic pulled out the broken katana blade, the jagged half still sharp. She could see signs that he was badly injured, and must have lost his guns, yet rage drove him every step forward.

"Die!" Trollic shouted, and he lunged forward, katana aimed to skewer them.

Before Toshi could raise his gun, Lotus stomped down on the ground with all her might, and the grass and soil beneath them gave way.

They fell—into the cave below—and Lotus landed on her feet and braced Toshi from hitting the floor.

Dirt continued to spill through the opening above their heads, and Trollic's raging bellow echoed down at them.

She pushed Toshi up against one of the tunnels leading from the cave and ran back to the hole in the ceiling.

Trollic was about to drop through.

The walls of the cave were weak and eroding.

Gathering all her strength into her right fist, she leaped straight up, fist forward, and blasted a second hole through the unstable ceiling.

As she fell back down and landed, the entire cave ceiling and tops of the walls started to collapse inward, groaning, clouds of sediment billowing.

Trollic vanished beneath the debris with one last roar, and she hurried to Toshi's side and pulled him down the tunnel with her as the tunnel's entrance folded in behind them.

After a fearful minute, the rumbling finally stopped, and the tunnel fell silent.

It was dark, reminding her of the storm drain, only the air was thin and smelled of earth. There was no going back. But the tunnel must lead to somewhere, eventually; it was a small island. Though, that wasn't very reassuring while trapped among the darkness and narrow walls.

She heard Toshi cough and squeezed his hand.

A faint glow appeared up ahead, so faint that she thought her eyes were imagining things in the dark. But then it grew brighter the farther they walked, and the tunnel walls around them fell away to a wide cavern.

There, glowing blue and soft at the center, stood a grand vertical pool: thin as a mirror and framed by a metallic contraption, its surface swirling without pause as if a finger continually stirred it.

"Is that...?" Lotus's jaw hung open, and she shared a look with Toshi.

He gaped, then broke into a grin, and clasped her hand more firmly in his.

She grinned back, a part of her feeling this must be a dream. The legend stood real and true before them.

The portal to another world. It was here, and they'd made it.

'Dad, I found it. I really found it!' Her other hand gripped the crystal pendant.

It hadn't been for nothing. Their sacrifices, their hope.

She looked again at Toshi, and he nodded knowingly.

Together, they approached the portal, step by step, pausing when the glassy surface came within an inch of their noses.

And then, holding in a deep breath, they stepped into the swirling blue, hand in hand, and felt their bodies leave the world behind.

Epilogue

Dad, I wish you and Mom could be here to see this. The Beorgan Society legend is true: we found the portal, and now we're living on Eartha, the second Earth, where there are countless races of Altered, all living freely and without any fear.

I'm not saying things are perfect—there are plenty of bad Altered as there are good—but it's different. I don't feel out of place. No one's hunting me down for my Healing power. People accept me. And there's no looming threat of war or global disasters—at least, not during the time I've been here.

I'd be lost without Toshi by my side. He's been my best friend, and so much more. I know why Lord God had us meet. He's helped me in so many ways, and says I've helped him, too. He still can't hear or speak well, but there's technology in this other world, and I'm hopeful that one day we'll find a solution.

We've already found one to Toshi's lost wing! He now has a fake wing and can glide through the skies as he used to. I'm so happy for him. I want him to take me up for a flight, sometime. Maybe on our honeymoon? That would be exciting. I should start planning that!

Dad, did you know there's a whole empire full of our race here? The Vemparic Empire, they call it, and the city is grander than anything I've ever seen! We took a trip there, and I'd like to go back and explore some more.

There are clans of hauk people said to live on the eastern continent. We'll have to go and find them, this summer. I know Toshi would enjoy spending time with his own kind, and it would help heal some of the past wounds he still carries.

In the meantime, I'm getting our newly bought cottage ready so we can move in after the wedding. Toshi is hard at work earning wages as a cobbler—you'd be amazed how good he is at making shoes! Who knew?

I work at the florist shop in town. It's a quaint little place in Bergvolk, a mountainous country. Sometimes I feel like I'm living in The Sound of Music! How I do miss those old movies. This world has its own stories and books, but occasionally I find some from our old world, too. Like the Three Musketeers, Beauty and the Beast, and a bunch of other fairy tales retold in altered versions.

Many cultures and languages here share resemblances to the world we left behind—as you'd expect—though there are clear differences, too. I'm glad it's not all so completely foreign from the ways of Earth. I couldn't survive something drastic like the planet Avatar.

Okay, I've journaled enough for today. I guess it's a good therapeutic exercise? Maybe my grandkids will read all this someday and think I'm a nut. My great legacy: Grandma Nutcase.

I should think up a legacy for Toshi…

Author's Note
& Trivia

What might the future look like around ninety years from now? It was fun imagining what new and advanced technologies we might have, such as huge drones flying the skies and transporting goods, and trains that travel on tracks through the air.

But while this story takes place in the future for us, it also takes place long before the timeline of the *Draev Guardians* series (*Strayborn*). As you read, Lotus arrives on planet Eartha back when the Vemparic Empire still existed—a time before The Disaster and the fight for the Pure Light power, back when the world was still unified.

Through this tale we can see how Earth and Eartha are connected and why their cultures and languages share many similarities. We also learn that not every Altered escaped to this new world, though. Many stayed behind to live here among us, and their varied standalone stories will be told through the *Alteredverse* series.

Books that take place on the twin planet are in the *Earthaverse* series, while books that take place in our world are the *Alteredverse* series. For example, *Beast of the Night* takes place in our world, and is therefore part of the *Alteredverse*.

To see the full Timeline of events, and where each book fits, visit the Bonus Material page in the Reader Insider Vault:

eerawls.com/reader-insiders

Now for some trivia!

I knew I wanted the story to take place in Japan, but I didn't want it to be the typical Tokyo scene. So, when I found beautiful Iki Island on the map, I knew that it was this southern area of Japan that I wanted to focus on.

All of the places mentioned in this book are real. There really is an underground mall, which in this futuristic tale has been abandoned and taken over by the mafia. Canal City is a fun shopping area, and the city park does have castle ruins. The pine grove along the coast that Lotus walks through, and even the Karatsu Burger food there, are real. The cemetery, too, though in this future it's become much larger than it is now. I added futuristic touches to many of the places throughout the story, while still keeping them recognizable.

Writing this book took a lot of time and research. I used maps and researched the entire route that Lotus and Toshi took from their city all the way to Iki Island. It was fun, and I learned a lot about this area of Japan and its culture.

I hope you enjoyed this adventure as much as I did writing it! Thank you for reading!

All thanks be to God, who makes me able. To learn more about Him, visit: **PeaceWithGod.net/where-is-god**

If you read Portal to Eartha and want to share it with other readers, please consider leaving a review on Amazon and Goodreads. This makes a huge difference for indie authors like me! Reviews help boost a book on retailer websites so that it'll be found by more readers.

You can be the first to learn about new releases, get bonus content, free ebooks and more by signing up for my newsletter at:

eerawls.com

Reader Insider Vault

Here You'll Get Access To:

- My Curated **No-Spice Book Lists**
- Bookish **News**, *Recs & Merch*
- **Behind the Scenes** details + First Looks + *Fun Bonuses* of my books
- **Free ebooks** & more!
- My **Exclusive Newsletter** & Substack: *where you can follow my author updates & fun random finds!*

eerawls.com

Scan QR Code:

THE ALTEREDVERSE

Books in the *Alteredverse* are standalone tales that take place in our world, at different points in time, and they often feature the humanoid Altered Ones.

They can be read in any order. Some books take place during our time, and some far into the future. To see the full Timeline of events, and where each book fits, visit the Reader Insider Vault's Bonus Material page:

eerawls.com/reader-insiders

If you enjoyed the world of *Portal to Eartha*, be sure to check out the other books in the *Alteredverse*. Also, check out the series **Draev Guardians** that takes place in the *Earthaverse* — the twin planet to our world (it can be read at any time and separately from *Alteredverse* books).

Suggested reading order:

- *Frost, Winter's Lonely Guardian*
- *Portal to Eartha*
- *Beast of the Night*
- *Madness Solver in Wonderland*

Frost, Winter Guardian and current resident of Boston.
For centuries he's watched over the winter seasons, and
now he longs to end his work and move on from this
world. But for that, he needs a replacement, and human
artist, Norah, might be the one, and the key to
thawing his icy heart.

Beast of the Night

A one-armed, practical girl. A rude lord hiding a curse. A dark secret with the town's fate hanging in the balance…

A Beauty and the Beast retelling with an Austrian twist

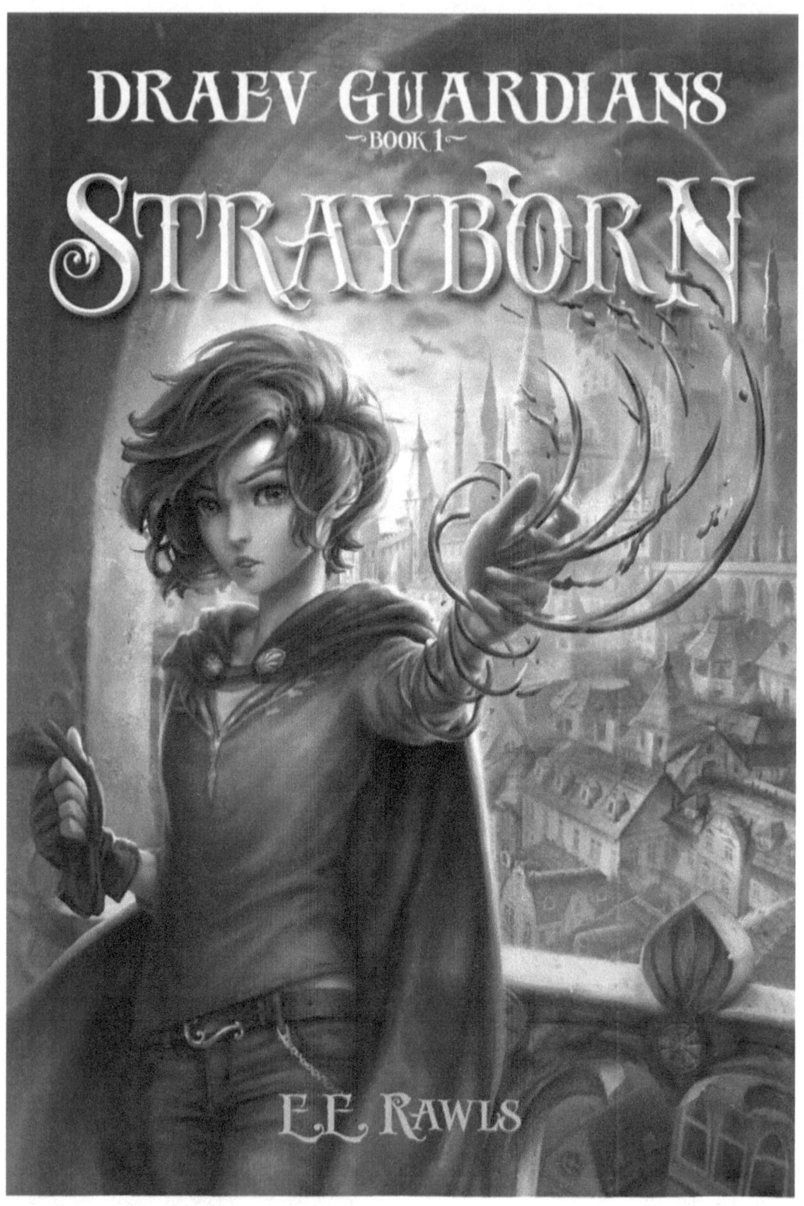

Elemental Manipulation is a tricky business as Cyrus, a girl who can manipulate metal, and Aken the last Scourgeblood, are about to find out, in a world that is determined to either use them or destroy them…
Welcome to the world of Eartha!

See all purchase links at eerawls.com

Madness Solver in Wonderland
"It's a crazy ride trying to keep the peace between both
Wonderland and Earth, solving mysteries, but somebody's
got to do it—and unfortunately that somebody is me.
Welcome to my nonsense life!"

How You Can Help

Reviews help boost a book on retailer websites so that it'll be found by more readers, which in turn helps support the author. *If you read Portal to Eartha and want to share it with other readers, please consider leaving a review on Amazon and Goodreads.* This makes a huge difference for indie authors like me! It doesn't have to be much, just click on how many stars you want to rate the book, and maybe add a sentence or two on your thoughts.

8 Ways to Support an Indie Author:

See a list of all the ways you can help support my work, as well as other indie authors!
Scan the QR code:

Author

E.E. Rawls is the product of a traveling family, who even lived in Italy for 6 years. She loves exploring the unknown, whether it be in a forest, the ruins of a forgotten castle, or in the pages of a book. Her brain runs on coffee, cuddly cats, and the mysterious beauty of nature while she writes.

Visit her online at **eerawls.com** and get free access to the Reader Insider Vault:

Reader Insider Vault

Here You'll Get Access To:
- My Curated **No-Spice Book Lists**
- Bookish **News**, *Recs & Merch*
- **Behind the Scenes** details + First Looks + *Fun Bonuses* of my books
- **Free ebooks** & more!
- My **Exclusive Newsletter** & Substack: *where you can follow my author updates & fun random finds!*

eerawls.com
Scan QR Code

www.ingramcontent.com/pod-product-compliance
Lightning Source LLC
Chambersburg PA
CBHW051927110726
47902CB00002B/446